*For Patrick, who is my very own
heart-squeezing Buster.
And without whom this
book wouldn't exist.*

First American Edition 2019
Kane Miller, A Division of EDC Publishing

Polly and Buster: The Wayward Witch & the Feelings Monster
Text & illustration copyright © 2017 Sally Rippin
Series design copyright © 2017 Hardie Grant Egmont
First published in Australia by Hardie Grant Egmont

Library of Congress Control Number: 2018958286

Printed and bound in the United States of America
3 4 5 6 7 8 9 10
ISBN: 978-1-61067-926-8

Polly AND Buster

The Wayward Witch & the Feelings Monster

written & illustrated by

SALLY RIPPIN

Kane Miller

A DIVISION OF EDC PUBLISHING

One

Polly Proggett is terrible at spells, which is rather unfortunate when you're a witch.

Today Polly's teacher is teaching the class how to make a potion to remove warts. Wart Removal is supposed to be one of the easiest spells in the book.

This time I'm going to make sure nothing goes wrong! thinks Polly.

Polly lines up the dusty jars of ingredients and marks them off in her book.

All I have to do is carefully follow the instructions in the spell book, just like Miss Spinnaker tells us to.

Miss Spinnaker is Polly's favorite teacher. She has curly red hair, which she knots into a messy bun at the top of her head, and she **jangles** with silver jewelry when she walks. Instead of the plain black school cape most of the Academy teachers wear, Miss Spinnaker wears a velvet cape embroidered with colorful threads and studded with little octagonal mirrors. The mirrors catch the sunlight as it slants through the high windows and send little dancing lights across the room.

Polly thinks Miss Spinnaker is glorious.

Miss Spinnaker has put Polly in a group with Rosemary and Valentine, who are very good at spells. Polly knows that Miss Spinnaker hopes some of their cleverness might rub off on her. Polly secretly hopes this might happen, too.

It's not that Polly isn't clever – as Miss Spinnaker always reassures her – it's just that things get muddled in Polly's head when she's given long and complicated instructions.

Is it three drops of toad juice next? Polly often wonders when she's in the middle of a spell. *Or a pinch of dried snake blood?*

And sometimes, when Polly looks at the yellowed pages of her leather-bound spell book, the letters seem to dance across the page. A letter *b* might suddenly look a lot like a *p*. A *W* might transform into an *m*.

Polly decides to be extra careful today. She watches Rosemary neatly tip three tablespoons of *milkwood sap* into her cauldron. The potion **bubbles** up and a perfect **puff** of smoke floats toward the ceiling.

Miss Spinnaker is walking around the classroom, handing out toads for everyone to practice on.

"Come along now, Polly," she says, as she approaches their table. "Have you started yet?"

Miss Spinnaker **plops** down three warty toads on the table.

Polly, Rosemary and Valentine quickly clap their hands over them before they leap away. Polly shudders when she feels the **bumpy, clammy** skin.

Rosemary picks up a pipette, dips it into

her bubbling potion, and squeezes the rubber bulb to fill up the glass tube. Then she squirts a drop of the potion onto one of her toad's biggest warts.

At first, the wart bubbles up into a clear blister, but then it **pops, shrivels** and **disappears.**

"Good work, Rosemary," Miss Spinnaker says, and wanders over to another table.

Polly peers down at the spell book again and chews the inside of her lip. She can't remember if she has already sprinkled in the newt crystals or if she is up to the bat flakes.

And does "tsp" mean tablespoon or teaspoon?

Polly is too embarrassed to ask Valentine.

Valentine is kind and sort of friendly, but Polly knows she will roll her eyes if she has to explain the recipe *again*. So Polly tosses in a handful of newt crystals, just in case. She figures it's better to have too much than not enough. Her potion bubbles up furiously, and Polly decides this means it's ready to use.

She squeezes up a big blob of liquid into her pipette and

squirts it onto her toad.

"Oh, look, look!" Polly says. "It's working!"

The warts on the toad's back begin to bubble up and blister.

8

"Good work, Polly!" Miss Spinnaker says as she hurries over, bracelets jangling.

But as they watch, the toad keeps on …

bubbling.
And bubbling
and bubbling,

until its slimy skin is just a great mass of warts.

"Ew!" Rosemary says, hopping backward in disgust. Her toad leaps off the table.

Malorie and Willow, who are working at the next bench, rush over to see what all the fuss is about. Willow slips on Rosemary's toad as it hops across the stone floor. She falls against Boris and Walter's table, and their cauldrons wobble precariously then crash to the ground.

The warlocks spring backward, but splashes of the foaming potion spray their trouser legs. Polly watches in horror as the uniform fabric dissolves where the potion has hit, and **splotches of warts begin sprouting on their legs.**

Malorie snorts in laughter. "Look what you've done, Polly! And now your toad is about ready to **explode!**"

And it's true. The poor creature is twice its size and has begun frothing at the mouth.

"Everyone! Look what Polly has done to her toad!" Malorie yells.

The other students rush over to Polly's table. Escaping toads leap about the classroom.

Polly feels a **fiery rage** boiling inside her. All Polly can see at that moment is mean Malorie Halloway, laughing her head off at Polly for ruining another potion, and before she can take a breath to calm herself, Polly has flung her loaded pipette full of wart potion at Malorie's face.

Polly gasps when she realizes what she has done. But of course, it is too late. Malorie's pretty skin is blistering into warts all over her face. Malorie claps her hands to her cheeks and screams.

At that precise moment, Polly's toad …

odes!

Bits of toad **splatter** everywhere.

"Enough!" roars Miss Spinnaker, sweeping a spell across the room to freeze everyone in their places.

Even the hopping toads are caught mid-flight and plop to the ground. The students stand fixed, eyes rolling toward their teacher, until she has released the spell and they can move again.

"Boris, Malorie, off to Matron's office," Miss Spinnaker says firmly. "She will fix you up. Walter, you too, if your legs have been affected. The rest of you, go back to your desks, quick smart, and continue on with your potions. I don't want to hear another peep out of a single witch or warlock for the rest of this lesson, is that clear?"

"Yes, Miss Spinnaker," the students mumble as they shuffle back to their desks, still giggling and picking bits of toad off their uniforms.

Malorie shoots Polly a **nasty** look as she leaves the classroom, whipping her long black plaits over her shoulders.

"And Polly," Miss Spinnaker sighs, "you will stay behind after class to clean up this mess."

"Yes, Miss Spinnaker," Polly says, her heart as heavy as a stone.

She has disappointed her favorite teacher yet again. No matter how hard she tries, Polly just can't seem to do anything right.

Two

Polly trudges out of the Academy grounds at the end of another long school day, her schoolbag heavy with textbooks and her new shoes smeary with toad.

Polly hates that she is so bad at spells. Nobody ever wants to be in a group with her. She messes up everything. Polly pretends she doesn't care that not a single witch at Miss Madden's

Academy of Witchcraft and Spells wants to be her friend, but secretly, deep down in that small place at the bottom of her tummy, she cares very much. Very, very much.

Lucky I have Buster, she reminds herself. *Buster doesn't mind if I am hopeless at everything. Buster likes me no matter what.* Buster is Polly's bestest, best friend in the whole wide world, which would truly be a wonderful thing if Buster were a witch or warlock.

But Buster is a monster.

Polly and Buster pretend they are not friends. After all, who has ever heard of a witch being friends with a monster? If Polly and Buster walk past each other in the street they don't even say hello. But every day, when Polly gets home, she dumps her schoolbag in the kitchen, kicks off her shoes and runs straight out into the backyard. She climbs to the top of the tree at the end of her yard.

Then she calls out,

"Awrooooo Awrooooo

OOOOOOOo.

OOOOO!"

This is their secret call.

Today, when Buster swings up into the tree, Polly sees he is wearing his favorite red overalls. They're a bit squeezy now that Buster has become so big and hairy, but they have lots of pockets. Buster fills his pockets with treasures for Polly to admire.

Buster tips out his pockets onto the branch. Today he has stones and sticks and three glass marbles. Then he digs his fingers even deeper and pulls out five sticky jamcakes covered in pocket fluff.

"Ta-da!" he says, grinning widely, his moss-green fur glowing pink with pride. "Afternoon tea!"

Polly smiles. "Thanks, Buster," she says, as cheerily as she can manage. She loves Buster's jamcakes,

even if they're covered in pocket fluff, but
she doesn't feel hungry today.
Polly sits and watches her
dearest friend shove one
jamcake after another
into his big, wet mouth.
Eventually Buster notices
that Polly isn't eating.
"Wash da madder?"
he asks, spraying crumbs
all over her. "Oopsh.
Shorry," he says.

He tries to wipe the crumbs off her face with his big paws but ends up smearing her cheeks with jam. "I mean," he says, swallowing a lump of jamcake, "what's the matter, Polly? You OK? You haven't touched your afternoon tea."

Polly stares off into the distance. "I messed up in spells today," she says sadly. "Again."

Buster stops chewing. "Oh," he says, looking concerned. "What happened?" He presses his finger down onto a **blob** of jam on his fur and sneaks it into his mouth.

Polly sighs. "I exploded a toad."

"Oh," Buster says again. He pauses, not quite sure what to say next. "Um, were you *supposed* to explode the toad?"

"No!" Polly says. "Of course not! I was supposed to get rid of its warts. But I accidentally exploded it instead."

Buster watches Polly carefully. She can see that he's wondering whether it's OK to laugh. Polly tries to keep her mouth still, but a smile twitches at the corner of her lips.

Buster lets out a hoot. "You exploded a *toad*?" he splutters. **"That's hilarious!"**

Polly frowns. "It's not funny, Buster," she says. "Malorie Halloway laughed at me. And then I got mad and threw wart potion at her face, and Boris and Walter got some on their legs, too, and now my mother will have to pay for new school pants for them, and Miss Spinnaker made me stay behind and clean up the whole classroom. It was the worst day ever!"

"Oh," says Buster. His face falls. "That's bad. That's really bad." He immediately shrinks in size.

When Buster feels happy he gets bigger and brighter. When he is sad he becomes small and gray. When Buster feels Polly's feelings he almost becomes the same size as her. Polly thinks this is the sign of a true friend.

Polly leans up against Buster. He feels warm and soft and comforting. Like a favorite blanket. "I don't know what's wrong with me," she says in a little voice. "Winifred is so good at spells. I'm hopeless at everything."

"No, you're not," Buster growls. He puts his arm around Polly and pulls her in tight. "You might not be good at spells and potions and all those other witchy things your show-offy big sister is good at. But you're much better at being a friend."

"Thanks, Buster," Polly says. She allows a **smile** to creep across her face.

"And you're much better at climbing trees," Buster says, grinning.

"That's not a very useful thing to be good at," Polly giggles.

"It is if you're a monster," Buster says. "Maybe you should come to my school and learn to be a monster?"

At Darklands School for Monsters, students get to climb as much as they like. Buster gets top marks for climbing. As well as climbing, they do **growling** and **crashing** and **crunching.** This always sounds like fun to Polly.

"I'd love that," she says, "but I do want to become a proper witch. A real Black Witch like Miss Spinnaker. Imagine! One that can do spells and make potions – and flies a broomstick.

I don't want to be an ordinary Green Witch like Mom, who prefers to drive a car and does her shopping at Witch Mart. My mom never does magic anymore. I mean, what's the point of studying witchcraft and spells at school if you never use it when you grow up?"

Buster shrugs. "Not every witch can be a Black Witch," he says. "But you'll be special at something, I just know it! And even if you never find that thing you are good at, you will always be special to me."

Polly feels her heart **squeeze** with love for Buster. She throws her arms around his big, thick waist. "You are the loveliest friend a witch could ever have."

"Aw," he mumbles, glowing scarlet with happiness. "Thanks, Polly."

"And you know what else? No matter how sad or grumpy or lonely I am, you always make me feel better. Always."

"Oh, stop!" Buster says. "Stop! Or I might explode!"

And it's true. Buster has grown so big and full of **happiness** that he is almost as tight as a balloon.

"Look at you!" Polly giggles. "You look like you could take off!"

At that moment a breeze blows through the trees and Buster lifts up from the branch.

"Buster!" Polly grabs his paw, shrieking with laughter. "Think of something sad. Quick! Or you'll float away!"

"I can't!" Buster bellows, growing bigger and lighter by the second. **"I'm too happy!"**

"Orphans!" Polly yells. "Little monsters who have lost their mommies!"

She watches Buster consider this terrible thought and sees his face buckle. Immediately he shrinks and becomes **heavier** and **darker**.

"Oh," he says in a deep voice. "That's sad."

And as Buster imagines for a moment what it would be like to have no mother, he shrinks, little by little, until he is almost his normal size again, and back to his usual shade of mossy green.

Polly gives him a big hug. "Do your friends at school know you can do that?" she asks.

Buster looks at her, horrified. "I'm a *monster*, Polly! Imagine if the other monsters knew.

I'd be teased so badly! I can never let them know how much I feel things. When I'm at school I have to concentrate hard to not feel anything at all. I can only be myself with you, Polly."

Polly leans right into Buster's chest and breathes in his **comforting** smell of leaves and wood smoke and moss. "It's the same for me, Buster," she murmurs, her heart full to bursting with happy sadness.

The two of them sit side by side on the long tree branch as the sky grows pink around them. Buster understands when Polly needs to be quiet. She closes her eyes and lets her thoughts drift around her like butterflies.

"Polly?" Buster whispers after a while.

"Mmmm?" Polly says, still leaning against him. She keeps her eyes closed.

"Polly?" Buster whispers again. A little louder this time.

"Is it important, Buster?" Polly says. "I'm kind of busy thinking."

Buster sighs deeply. A big, growling, sort of longing sigh.

Polly opens one eye, then the other. It's almost dark anyway. Her mom will be calling her in for dinner soon. "What is it?" She smiles at her friend.

Buster smiles back **wonkily** and clears his throat. He shifts his bottom along the branch. "Um. I was wondering ... I mean, I've just been thinking –"

Polly puts her hand on his big paw. She can see he is turning pink with shyness. "It's OK, Buster. You can tell me anything, you know. You're my best friend."

"Weeellll ..." he begins, turning pinker still. "I was just wondering. Are you going to eat that last jamcake?"

Three

That night at dinner, Polly's mom serves up Polly's least-favorite food.

"Mealworms!" she moans. "Do we have to have mealworms again?"

"Mealworms are good for you," says her mom, pouring herself a glass of juniper wine. "They're full of iron."

Next to Polly, Winifred takes an extra-large helping of mealworms and dumps them on her plate. She smiles sweetly at Polly. Polly knows her sister doesn't like mealworms much either, but Winifred loves any opportunity to make Polly look bad.

This is not hard. Winifred is good at everything. Polly is good at nothing.

Winifred has changed out of her school uniform into shiny pink leggings and her favorite spider-print top. Her long, glossy hair is twisted up into a high ponytail with complicated loops and sparkly clips and bows. Polly is still in her crumpled school uniform of a gray tunic and stripy leggings. Polly can't get through a day without putting a hole in her expensive woolen stockings, so her mom lets her wear leggings to school instead. Already her knees are smudged brown and green from her afternoon in the tree. Her knotty black hair is full of sticks and leaves.

Polly pushes a mealworm around in the sauce with her fork. It **curls** into a ball.

"Ew, this one's not even dead yet," Polly **grimaces**.

Her mom smiles. "Fresh from the market. I've found an old ogre woman who collects them herself. They're much better for you than the dried ones."

Polly feels her tummy **churn**. From the corner of her eye she watches her big sister munching away. Polly helps herself to the thistles and kale from the salad bowl and pours some betel nut oil over them.

Greens aren't her favorite either, but at least they don't move.

She jabs her fork into the leaves, careful to avoid any mealworms that might have crawled under, before she puts some in her mouth.

"Can I please have some more mealworms?" Winifred asks, pushing her plate forward.

"Of course!" their mom says, happily. "How are you doing with yours, Polly?"

"Fine," Polly sighs, hiding a **wriggling** pile of the slime-covered grubs under a thistle leaf.

Polly feels something soft and wet against her knee. It's Gumpy, their pet bortal. She's squatting beside Polly, drooling and looking up at her with hopeful eyes.

Gumpy loves mealworms. But then, Gumpy loves any food. In fact, Gumpy will eat just about anything you feed her. When Polly and Winifred were younger, they tested this out. They tried easy things at first: paper, string, clay, bubble wrap.

Gumpy had eaten all of them without a fuss.

So then they tried crunchy things that were a little harder to chew. Batteries, teacups, a Slinky, and even their mother's glasses case. With her glasses still in it.

This last one got them into trouble because their mother's glasses were new. Ever since then, Polly and Winifred have been banned from feeding her.

Besides, Gumpy's a little on the roly-poly side now, so she's only supposed to eat special bortal diet food. This makes her cranky and hungry all the time, so they have to be extra careful not to leave anything on the floor. The week before, Gumpy had forced her way into Polly's bedroom while she was at school, and devoured her whole set of *My Little Unicorn* figurines.

The only good thing about having a pet who eats everything is that Polly's mom never has to sweep the floor. Anything that falls onto it is vacuumed up within minutes.

When no one is looking, Polly scoops up a forkful of mealworms and drops them under the table.

"Mom! Polly's feeding Gumpy!" Winifred sings out.

"Polly!" says their mom.

"Winifred!" growls Polly. "You're such a tattletale!"

"Eat your mealworms," says their mom.

"I'm not hungry," Polly grumbles.

"Maybe that's because of all the jamcakes you ate with Buster?" Winifred says, smiling sweetly.

"Have you been spying on me?" Polly shouts.

"Why would I *spy* on you?" Winifred says. "I can see you from my bedroom window, **bug brain**. Don't worry, you're not *that* interesting!"

"Polly," their mom sighs, pouring herself another glass of juniper wine. She pushes her glasses up onto her head and rubs the bridge of her nose. "You're not still playing with that monster from next door, are you? You *know* witches don't play with monsters. It was OK when you were younger, but not now you're growing up. Imagine what the other witches at school would think!"

"But he's my best friend," Polly says, **angrily**. Then, a little quieter, "My only friend. None of the witches at school like me."

"It's true," Winifred says, pushing her empty plate away and picking at her black nail polish. "She has no friends."

"Winifred!" their mom says. "That's not very nice. I'm sure that's not true."

"It is!" Polly says. She stabs at a mealworm with her fork. "Nobody wants to be friends with me. I'm hopeless at everything. Especially spells."

"She threw wart potion at Malorie Halloway

in class today," Winifred says, sniggering.

"Polly!" their mom gasps. "Not Deidre Halloway's daughter?"

Polly nods.

"Oh, Polly! Why?" their mom groans. "Anyone but Deidre Halloway's daughter. I'll *never* hear the end of it at the next Committee meeting."

"She was laughing at me!" Polly says.

"That doesn't mean you should ..." Their mother throws her hands in the air. "Oh, Polly. You really do have to try harder to manage your temper. You're *so* like your Aunt Hilda ..."

This is what it always comes to. Every time Polly's mom despairs of Polly, she throws her hands up into the air and says, "You're just like your Aunt Hilda."

Aunt Hilda is their father's wild and wayward sister. She ran away at sixteen in a haze of secrecy and scandal, and was never seen again. Polly's mother never talks about Aunt Hilda in a good way. To be compared to Aunt Hilda is just about the worst thing Polly's mother can say. Polly feels her throat bunch up and her eyes spring with tears. She pushes her chair back from the table.

"Polly! Where are you going?" her mother asks as Polly stands up.

"Outside!" says Polly.

"I'll bet she's going next door," Winifred smirks. "Do you want me to stop her?"

"Just leave her," their mother sighs, as Polly rushes out the front door and into the darkness. Her heart is **hurting** and her eyes are stinging and there is only one person in the world who can make her feel better.

Four

Polly runs through the **star-speckled** gloom, along their neat garden path lined with nodding clawflowers, out the tall black iron gates and along the street until she reaches the identical black gates of the house next door. She creaks them open and her sodden heart lifts a little when she sees the welcoming glow coming from the windows of Buster's crumbling old mansion.

It's been a while since Polly has visited Buster's family. These days, she and Buster can only meet secretly. Luckily, the old morpett tree that leans up against the high stone wall between their two houses is the perfect spot.

But when Polly was little, she spent almost as much time at Buster's house as her own – especially after her dad died. Sometimes, during that long, sad winter, Polly's mom wouldn't get out of bed, not even to eat the soup that Buster's mom had cooked for her. When Polly and Winifred's mother was ghost-like with grief, and only just floating through each day as best as she could, Polly and her big sister would go over to Buster's house. The three of them would play hidey or hunt snails in the ramshackle garden. They would perch up at the kitchen counter and dip jamcakes fresh from the oven into bowls of warm honeyed milk.

Now that Winifred is thirteen and head witch in her class, she wouldn't be seen dead with a monster.

Polly strides up the crooked stone path that cuts through Buster's overgrown yard. She knocks on the enormous wooden door. Heavy footsteps approach and the porch lantern is switched on.

"Oooh, it's Polly!" Buster's mom squeals happily.

She stretches out her big knotty hands and scoops Polly up into her arms. Buster's mother is not the most attractive monster in town, but when she smiles it's like the sun is shining right out of her.

Buster appears in the hallway behind his mother.

"**Mom! Be careful!**" he says protectively. "She's not a monster, you know!"

Buster's mother plonks Polly back down on the stone porch and flattens her ruffled hair with her big, calloused fingers.

"Oh, look how big you're getting!" she coos. "How are you, my little **witchling?** It's so nice to see you!"

"I'm OK," Polly says, laughing and wiping something sticky off her cheek. "It's nice to see you too, Mrs. Grewclaw."

"Oh, you know to call me Patsy, my dear smootchkin!" she cries. "No need for formalities between us. **Bruce!** Look who's here! It's Polly, from next door. Buster's little witch friend!"

"Well, bring 'er in!" Buster's dad roars from the other room. "Don't leave her standing out in the cold!"

Patsy rolls her eyes. "As if I'd do that," she says, placing her hands on her broad hips and shaking her head. "Come inside, **munchky.** Have you eaten? We're having a cheeky flummery cake in the drawing room, if you'll join us?"

Polly's tummy rumbles with pleasure. She was happy to have avoided eating the mealworms at dinner, but now she realizes how hungry she is. "Yes, please!" she says.

"Are you all right?" Buster whispers, as Polly steps inside and his mother closes the door behind them. He has turned a little gray with **worry.**

Polly shrugs. "I just needed to get out of the house for a while. Is that OK?"

"Of course!" Buster's mother says. "As long as you don't mind a bit of company? We have a few monsters staying with us at the moment. But there's plenty of room for more!"

Polly smiles. Patsy is always looking after

other monsters. Sometimes
they are baby monsters
who are naughty and
troublesome. They climb
into cupboards and eat all
the food, mess up the house and
break her best crockery. Other times
they are old, broken monsters with worn-down
teeth, bent over with sadness from never having
been loved. The old ones are cranky and fill up
the room with dampness and smell.

"They're driving Dad nuts," Buster tells Polly.
"As usual."

"Well, someone has to look after them, don't
they?" his mother says, turning to walk down

the corridor toward the back of the house. "It's all very well to love monsters who are loveable, but it's the unlovable ones who need it the most."

Polly and Buster follow Patsy down the dark hallway, careful not to trip over all the junk that has collected there. Generations of Buster's relatives peer down at them from ornate wooden frames hung crookedly along the walls. At the entrance to the drawing room, Patsy kicks a massive pair of leather boots to one side and leads them in.

A **higgledy-piggledy** collection of old armchairs has been moved into a semicircle around the enormous fireplace, where flames hiss and roar. Buster's father, Bruce, is leaning over a low table where a towering flummery cake teeters precariously on a pretty china plate.

It is topped with bilberries and slathered with cream.

Bruce is lanky and skinny and only half Patsy's height. He has scaly skin, not fur, and a huge hooked nose that Buster was lucky not to have inherited. Bruce looks permanently cross and frowny, unlike Buster's sunshiny mother. But even though he grumbles about her all day long, there is no one in the world who adores Patsy more than Bruce does. Even if she does fill the place with all manner of annoying monsters who eat them out of house and home.

This evening, there are three old monsters by the fire, crammed into the threadbare floral armchairs. Each monster is balancing a little china plate with a big wedge of flummery cake on their wobbly knees. When one monster opens his mouth to pop a forkful of cake in, a **great gust of stinky air** rolls out.

Polly has to wipe away the tears that spring into her eyes and stop herself from gagging.

"Bernie hasn't eaten in a while. It makes his breath a little stinky, I'm afraid," Patsy whispers to Polly and Buster. "How's the cake, Bernie?" she calls out to the old monster.

Bernie nods happily and gives them a great gap-toothed grin. Another wave of fetid air rushes toward them. He lifts the china plate and licks the cream off it with a big pink tongue.

Then he makes to pop the plate in his mouth, too.

"Oh no! Not the plate, please, dear," Patsy says, rushing over to Bernie's side. "I'm a bit short on crockery as it is. Here, have some more tea instead. Charlie, Graham, would you like some more, too? Polly! Come over, **pippikin,** and have some cake. You can sit on the footstool in front of the fire. Don't worry, they don't bite. Oh, except Maggie. But only if she's startled. Maybe don't sit too close to her."

Polly heads toward the fireplace with Buster and turns to look at the monster Patsy is referring to. Maggie sits on her own in a dark corner, scowling and grunting, her bony knees tucked up under her chin. When she sees Polly looking at her, she **hisses** and sticks out a long purple tongue at them.

"Maggie's family kicked her out because she kept biting the grandchildren," Patsy explains in hushed tones. "Poor dear. Now she has nowhere to go."

"Just as well we don't have any grandchildren in the house," Bruce grumbles. "Cake, dear?" he says, handing Polly a plate.

Polly and Buster sit side by side on the little

footstool by the fire, scoffing Patsy's glorious cake. "Oh, this is so yummy!" Polly sighs, licking cream off her fingers. "I wish my mom would make cakes like this. She only lets us eat healthy sweets, like chickweed tart and wormwood loaf."

"Well, your mother has always been a lot more ... *conscientious* ... about her cooking than I am," Patsy says tactfully.

"Do you want another piece?" Buster asks.

Polly rubs her tummy, where three pieces of flummery cake are now digesting, and **burps.** The monsters in the room all roar appreciatively.

Polly giggles. "No, I'd better get back soon.

Mom will be worried about me."

"Do say hello to your ma, dear," Patsy says. "And tell her that cup of tea I promised over the fence all those years ago is still on offer!"

"I will," says Polly, even though she will do no such thing.

Polly knows her mother would be more likely to fly to the moon than be seen sharing a pot of tea with a monster. Witches just don't mix with monsters. Especially witches like Polly's mom who care a great deal about what other witches think of them.

"Buster, you'll see Polly home, won't you?" Patsy says. "And keep an eye out for Maggie, dear. She must have slipped outside while we were eating. I don't *think* she'd bite Polly, but it's probably better to be on the safe side."

Five

When Polly gets home, the kitchen has been cleared and the dishwasher is on. Only Gumpy is still under the table, helpfully vacuuming up any last crumbs that have spilled or mealworms that have escaped. Polly wonders if she is going to be in trouble for not helping clear the table. It was her job to stack the dishwasher tonight.

She can hear the TV on in the family room.

She tiptoes down the hallway, deciding it's probably better to avoid her mom for now, just in case.

"Polly?" her mom calls out. "Is that you?"

Her mother's voice sounds tired but friendly. Polly's not in trouble. She sighs in relief.

"Come and sit with us for a bit, **pumpkin**," her mom calls. "We're watching *Nastiest Witch on the Block*. Sycamore is winning."

Polly's mom is curled up on their neat linen couch, her uncomfortable black work heels kicked off. Winifred is on the beanbag in front of the television.

Polly hovers in the doorway of the family room to watch. The aim of *Nastiest Witch on the*

Block is to see who can be the meanest to the other contestants. Polly's mom and Winifred are hooked on it, but it's not really Polly's thing.

A commercial comes on and Winifred unglues her eyes from the TV and twists around to look at Polly. **"How was Buster?"** she taunts, but to Polly's surprise, their mother ignores her.

"Come along, pumpkin," their mom beckons, smiling.

She pats the space beside her, a glass of juniper wine in her other hand.

Polly wanders over and curls into her mother's side on the couch. Her mom smells like vanilla and spiderwebs and juniper berries.

"Don't mind your sister," she whispers in Polly's ear. "She doesn't mean any harm. She's just going through a stage."

Gumpy trots in, plops down on the shaggy rug and within moments is snoring loudly.

Their mother turns up the volume, and they watch the commercial where a witch demonstrates the fancy new gadgets on the Broomstick 100.

"I can't wait to get my broomstick license," Winifred says enviously.

"Broomsticks are dangerous," tuts their mother.

"Mom!" Winifred groans. "All my friends will be getting one! They're fine."

"Well, I certainly don't like those motorized ones. There are just too many accidents each year for me to feel comfortable with my daughters riding them."

"It's only **bat-brained** warlocks who fly too fast who have accidents," says Winifred.

"We'll talk about this again when you're sixteen," their mom says, shutting down the conversation just as their show comes back on.

The three of them settle in to watch. It's getting close to the season finale, and only Sycamore and three other contestants remain. Sycamore is an old schoolmate of Polly's mother, and the most horrible witch they've had on so far.

"Ooh, she's good, isn't she?" Polly's mom says.

They watch Sycamore cast a spell on another contestant, which makes her break out into pus-filled sores just as she's about to go on a date.

"She was always so good at spells at school," continues their mom. "I'm not surprised she's kept up with it. Not many other witches in our class did."

Sycamore's latest victim bursts into tears and runs away from the restaurant where her date is waiting.

Winifred guffaws with laughter. "That silly witch will be voted off this week, for sure!"

Polly has an **uneasy** feeling in her stomach. She doesn't know what's wrong with her. Everyone at her school loves this show. Sycamore is the pride of Miss Madden's Academy of Witchcraft and Spells, and was voted *Most Powerful Witch* in her final year. But when Polly watches the poor witch standing there, with tears flowing over her bumpy, sore-covered cheeks, it just makes her feel confused.

Polly knows it's only a game, and that the losing witches will have their spells reversed the moment they leave the show. But she doesn't find any of it funny like everyone else seems to. If anything, it only makes her sad.

"Actually, I've just remembered I've got homework to do," Polly mumbles.

"OK, dear," her mother says, her eyes still fixed on the screen, "but don't stay up too late, will you? You've got a field trip to the gallery tomorrow and you don't want to be tired."

Polly trudges upstairs to her room, **heavyhearted**, once again wondering why she feels so different from everyone she knows.

Six

The next morning when Polly wakes up, the sun is streaming through her window. Polly feels sure this means it's going to be a good day.

Just to be on the safe side, she takes exactly five hops to get to her wardrobe to put on her uniform. She knows it's eleven hops from her wardrobe to the bathroom. She tells herself if she only does an odd number of hops all morning until breakfast, then this will be a one-hundred-percent guarantee that nothing will go wrong. How could it, on a day as **chirpy** and **sunny** as this?

But when she gets to the bathroom door, Winifred is in there. Polly **wobbles** a little in the doorway on one foot. She puts her other foot down slowly, carefully, just the toe point, so she is not exactly standing, but not exactly hopping either.

It is too late. Winifred has seen.

"Are you hopping?" she sneers.

"No," says Polly quickly.

"Mom!" Winifred yells. "Polly is doing that hopping thing again."

"Don't do the hopping thing, Polly," their mom calls out in her tired-and-not-really-interested voice.

What she is really saying is that it's way too early for her to be dealing with their arguments.

"I'm not!" Polly yells.

"She is!" Winifred yells.

"That's enough!" their mom yells out from the bottom of the stairs. "Get dressed and come downstairs for breakfast. Right. Now."

"Why do you care anyway?" Polly hisses.

She turns around and tries to hop away from her sister with as much dignity as she can manage.

"You're weird!" Winifred snarls. "And you're embarrassing! How do you think it feels being sister to the weirdest witch at school?"

"Three, four, five ..." Polly counts, ignoring her.

All she has to do is make it to the top of the stairs in nine hops, then she can slide down the bannister and her made-up spell will be complete. She may not be good at real spells, but that doesn't mean she can't invent a few of her own.

"Six, seven, eight ..."

She is almost at the stairs.

She reaches for the bannister, but before she can touch the wood, her standing foot is knocked out from under her and she tumbles onto the carpet.

"Winifred!" she yells. "Why are you so mean? Now you've ruined everything!"

"Mom said to stop," Winifred says, her eyes narrowing to slits.

Then she marches back to the bathroom, slamming the door behind her.

Polly rubs at the carpet burn on her knee. Hot tears prickle her eyes. She pulls herself up with the help of the bannister, but even with her last wobbly hop, she knows her happy-day spell is ruined. As if to confirm her fears, a dark cloud rolls slowly across the sky and the jolly patch of sunlight on the landing disappears.

She slides slowly down the bannister, Gumpy galumphing beside her.

The family sits down to breakfast. Polly picks unenthusiastically at her mother's homemade muesli of dried lizard flakes and bark shavings, then collects her lunch box from the kitchen counter. Even without peering inside, she knows her mother will have packed something healthy for them like **boiled snake eggs** and pickled herring. Or last night's leftover mealworms with wilted greens.

She wishes she could just occasionally have a simple pumpkin-paste sandwich and a pack of turnip chips, like the other witches in her class.

Winifred marches ahead of Polly to the bus

stop. Buster is already waiting there, his great big bottom taking up almost all of the space on the bench. When Winifred stands in front of him, her hands on her hips, Buster jumps up apologetically so that she can sit down.

"Sorry about my sister," Polly mumbles as she sidles up beside him.

"That's OK," he grins kindly. "I was tired of sitting anyway."

He makes a big show of stretching out his stumpy legs.

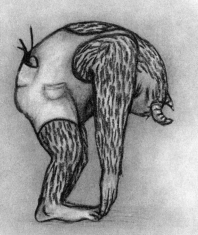

Despite Polly's heavy heart, Buster looks so ridiculous she can't help giggling.

Encouraged by her laughter and hidden from view behind the bus shelter, Buster launches into a full exercise routine, complete with

jumping jacks, twists and

jogging
in place.

When he bends over to touch his toes he **tumbles** right over, and Polly **snorts** with **delight.**

"Polly!" Winifred warns from where she is seated on the other side of the shelter.

Polly claps her hand across her mouth, her shoulders **jiggling** up and down with laughter.

"Stop it!" she giggles, pulling Buster to his feet and brushing dirt off his big hairy knees. "The bus is coming!"

Buster gives Polly a quick hug before the bus is close enough for them to be seen. "In the tree?" he asks.

"At half past three," Polly answers. **"Just you and me?"**

"As it'll always be," Polly assures him, as always.

Then Buster stands to one side to let the witches get on first, just as his mother has taught him. And just as his mother taught him, he is careful to pick a seat at the back with the other monsters – not in front, where the witches like to sit.

After all, a monster must always know their place.

Seven

Polly has her field trip first thing that morning, so after roll call the students pile excitedly into the big school bus to make their way to the National Gallery. Nobody ever chooses to sit next to Polly, but today she doesn't mind.

She is quite happy to sit up at the front with Miss Spinnaker.

"How's your art assignment coming along?" Miss Spinnaker asks Polly as the bus rumbles along the bumpy streets.

They pass the Town Hall and the markets and the crumbling factories, where the lowliest monsters toil for twelve-hour days, cracking rocks and shoveling earth to uncover the gems and stones and crystals that will be ground up for witches to use in their potions.

"Good!" Polly says. **"I love art."**

"And you are very good at it," Miss Spinnaker says kindly.

"I wish I was better at spells," Polly sighs. "I just find it so hard to follow the instructions."

It doesn't occur to her to tell Miss Spinnaker

about the way the words seem to dance across the page. Polly assumes it's the same for everyone. As far as she is aware, all the other students in the class are just better at focusing. Polly finds it impossible to concentrate on her work if there is something even mildly interesting going on outside the classroom window. She so easily slips into daydreaming about climbing trees, or fishing in creeks, or picking bilberries in the woodlands with Buster.

Only in art class can Polly truly lose herself in her work.

"You'll get there," Miss Spinnaker assures her. "With a little practice. And a little patience and coolheadedness too, perhaps?" she says, raising her eyebrows to remind Polly of yesterday's debacle.

Malorie's skin is completely clear again today, but she still shot Polly a nasty look as they boarded the bus.

Polly grimaces. "I know. I just get so mad when people laugh at me. I'm trying my hardest!"

"It's OK, Polly," Miss Spinnaker says gently, resting her bangled hand on Polly's arm. "Spell making and potion brewing comes naturally to some witches, so they don't understand why others find it so difficult. Don't let a little teasing ruffle you, Polly. I had to work very hard at school to do well at spells. It didn't come naturally to me either."

"Really?" says Polly. "But you're so good!"

"I practiced every day," Miss Spinnaker says. "Harder than any other student. And in the end, I got top marks in my Witch Finals. That's partly why I've made a career out of teaching spells. I worry that spell making and potion brewing will die out. Witches and warlocks don't seem as interested in the traditional ways of life. It's all motorized broomsticks and microwave potions these days. My grandmother would turn in her grave if she knew. Look! Like that!" she says, pointing at a smart new Broomstick Stallion in silver **ZOOMING** dangerously past them.

It easily overtakes the cars and the buses and

the old-fashioned wooden broomsticks putting along beside them.

Miss Spinnaker shakes her head in disapproval, and her earrings jangle.

Finally, the bus pulls up outside the gallery. The witches and warlocks squeal with the excitement of being out of school for the whole morning.

"Students," Miss Spinnaker warns, "you are representing Miss Madden's Academy at all times so your behavior must be exemplary. You know the rules. No running and no shouting in the gallery and, most importantly, no spells whatsoever outside of school grounds. Do I make myself clear?"

"Yes, Miss Spinnaker," the students chime, fidgeting in their seats, desperate to get off.

"Polly, you will head the line with Malorie," Miss Spinnaker instructs.

Polly flashes Miss Spinnaker a look. She is thrilled to be chosen to head the line – but with Malorie? She doesn't have to look at Malorie to know she would be grimacing, too.

"Can't I be with Willow or Rosemary?" says Malorie, rolling her eyes. "Or even Harold?"

Malorie grabs the hand of the closest warlock to prove she would rather be paired with *anyone* other than Polly. Harold looks thrilled to have been singled out by Malorie, and his ruddy cheeks blush pink. Willow and Rosemary giggle.

"You and Polly will head the line," Miss Spinnaker repeats, "and to make up for the chaos you *both* created in yesterday's spells class, you can work together as a pair today."

"What?" Malorie says. "I didn't do anything! Polly threw wart potion at *me!*"

"You were being mean!" Polly scowls.

"I can pair with Polly," Valentine says.

She tucks her curly black hair behind her ears and smiles shyly at Polly.

Even though Polly knows Valentine is being kind, this only makes her feel worse. *Why can't Miss Spinnaker just let me work on my own?* she thinks crossly.

"Thank you, Valentine, but I think it will

be good for both Polly and Malorie to work together. Who knows? You witches might be surprised at what you can learn from each other."

Malorie **huffs,** then tosses her plaits over her shoulder and pushes past Polly to be first off the bus.

Polly steps off after her into the pale autumn sunshine, the crisp morning air on her cheeks. Dried leaves swirl at her feet like crazy dancers, and despite being teamed up with Malorie for the morning, Polly feels a sudden surge of happiness. Autumn is her favorite time of the year. And the art gallery is her favorite place to visit. *Maybe things aren't so bad after all,* she tells herself.

But when another school bus turns into the gallery parking lot, Polly gets a familiar feeling of dread in the pit of her stomach. The tips of her fingers tingle and she knows right down in her bones that something awful is going to happen.

Please don't let that bus be from Darklands, Polly thinks.

But already she knows that it is.

Eight

"That's not *monsters* on that bus, is it?" Malorie says, curling up her pretty button nose in disgust.

Polly clutches Malorie's arm to pull her toward the gallery, but Malorie has already turned to Willow and Rosemary, who are standing right behind them.

"**Ew**," Willow grimaces. "It is! It is!"

Malorie, Willow and Rosemary stop in their tracks, blocking the whole line of students behind them. Everyone is now turning to look at the old gray bus hissing and wheezing its way into the parking lot.

Polly stares straight ahead.

Miss Spinnaker, who is still organizing the stragglers into two neat lines, comes over to see what all the fuss is about.

"*Monsters,* Miss Spinnaker," Malorie sneers. "What are they doing letting monsters visit the gallery on the same day as *us*?"

"Monsters have every right to visit the gallery, just as witches and warlocks do," Miss Spinnaker says firmly. "Those monsters are from Darklands. They must have a gallery field trip today, too."

Malorie makes a face as the first monsters stumble their way noisily out of the bus. They spot the line of witches and sneer and guffaw.

"Witches! Warlocks!" growls the biggest monster. **"Ew!"**

"Come along, students," Miss Spinnaker says. "You don't have to associate with them, but there's no need to be rude, either. Remember our Academy manners."

When Miss Spinnaker's back is turned, Polly sees Malorie stick her tongue out at the monster who just spoke. He crosses his eyes at Malorie and snorts with laughter.

Polly pulls Malorie forward, her heart **leaping** about in her chest.

"Come on," she says, irritably. "It's cold out here. Let's get inside!"

There is one monster from Darklands she doesn't want to see. Not now, anyway.

Miss Spinnaker ushers everyone into the

gallery and straight up to the second floor. Polly starts to feel her breathing return to normal, and once they are surrounded by paintings she knows and loves, she almost begins to enjoy herself again.

Polly walks beside Malorie, their clipboards in hand, and together the two of them go through the list of questions Miss Spinnaker has given them. The exhibition is titled:

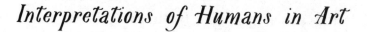

Interpretations of Humans in Art

In the first question, their teacher has asked them to list ten different humans from well-known myths and legends. Polly writes down Hedrid, the human who steals witch babies, Augustus, the leader of witch burnings, and Pyralosis, the human who hides at the bottom of swamps, waiting to suck down any unsuspecting witch, warlock or monster child who might wander by. All horrible humans indeed!

Polly is slow at reading, which makes her slow at writing, too. In the time it has taken her to write down three human myths and agonize over her spelling, Malorie has already completed her list and is on to the next page.

Malorie is always the quickest to finish her work.

Polly skips a few myths to catch up with her.

"Oh no," Malorie grumbles. "We have to draw a picture of a human from one of these paintings. I hate drawing."

She flops down onto the long padded bench in the middle of the brightly lit room. Other witches and warlocks wander around in pairs, studying the paintings and jotting down notes on their clipboards.

Polly perches on the bench next to her and studies the painting in front of them. It is of a group of monsters having a picnic in a beautiful forest. But when Polly looks closely, she sees it's not just monsters at the picnic. There are witches in the group, too!

The witches are laughing and sharing food, as though it's perfectly normal to have a picnic with monsters. Polly knows that this was the Olden Days, but it makes her happy to see them all sitting together. She wishes it was still like that today.

Polly begins by sketching some monsters, then the witches. She feels Malorie watching over her shoulder.

"You're good," Malorie says.

Polly feels **happy butterflies** bloom in her chest. "Thanks," she says. "I love drawing."

Malorie watches her for a little longer. "You're *really* good. I'm terrible at drawing. I can't even draw a stick figure."

She shows Polly her drawing. Polly is surprised to see that Malorie isn't lying. It really isn't very good. And Polly thought Malorie was good at everything!

"I can help, if you like?" Polly suggests shyly.

"Really?" Malorie says. "Thanks! Hey, maybe I can answer your questions and you can do my drawings?"

"That's a great idea!" says Polly.

She smiles at Malorie, and Malorie smiles back. Polly is surprised at how pretty Malorie looks when she smiles.

Polly finishes her drawing and then starts work on Malorie's.

"Gosh," Malorie says, enviously, "do you think you could teach me how to draw one day?"

"**Sure,**" says Polly, unable to hide how thrilled she feels.

"Great!" says Malorie. Then she stands and wanders over to look more closely at the other paintings in front of them. "Humans look pretty spooky, don't they? Do you think they really exist?"

"I don't know," Polly shrugs. "There are lots of stories about them."

"My mom says they are just made up to scare

little children," Malorie says, twirling a plait in her fingers. "She doesn't believe in humans."

"Neither does mine," Polly says. "But my dad did."

"Really?" says Malorie. Then she pauses. "*Did?* You mean, he doesn't believe in them anymore?"

"No," says Polly, looking back down at her drawing, "I mean, he died. Five years ago. In the mine accident."

"Oh. I'm sorry," Malorie says, coming back over to Polly and sitting down next to her. "I didn't know. My uncle did, too. My mom's brother. She still misses him. Sorry about your dad, though. That must be awful."

"That's OK," Polly says.

She wants to change the subject now. Talking about her dad makes her uncomfortable. She doesn't like the thought of anyone feeling sorry for her because she doesn't have a dad. Lots of witches, warlocks and monsters lost their parents in the accident, not just her.

"Here, I've finished our drawings," she says, standing up and handing Malorie back her clipboard. "Let's go into the next room."

The two witches continue wandering through the gallery, chatting about ordinary things: clothes, cute warlocks from school, and whether they'll earn their witch hats at the end of the year.

Polly is pretty sure she won't.

"Yes, you will," Malorie assures her. "You just need to practice your spells. Maybe I can help you? In return for you helping me with my drawing?"

"Really?" Polly asks.

"As long as you promise not to throw any more potions at me," says Malorie, smiling.

"OK!" Polly giggles, and she feels **a warm ball of happiness** heat her up from the inside. Her cheeks burn pink with delight.

Nine

"All right, students," Miss Spinnaker calls, clapping her hands to get everyone's attention. "I hope you've all brought a snack with you? You have twenty minutes to eat something and use the bathroom. We will then meet at the front entrance to catch the bus back to school. Is everyone clear on what we are doing?"

"Yes, Miss Spinnaker," the students chorus, dashing off in different directions to make the most of this last moment of freedom.

"Stay with your partners!" Miss Spinnaker calls after them, but Polly doesn't need to be told twice. She's not letting Malorie out of her sight.

"Let's go to the bathrooms downstairs," says Malorie, when they see the line in front of the witches' room.

She grabs Polly's hand, and they walk to the stairs as fast as they can without actually running. Once they are in the stairwell, Malorie pulls Polly into a run and they race down the steps, two by two.

Polly giggles with the excitement of dashing around the gallery with her new *almost* friend.

"Oh!" Malorie says, stopping so suddenly that Polly crashes into her. **"Monsters!"**

Polly peers over Malorie's shoulder and sees the huddle of Darklands monsters moving toward them, clipboards in hand.

"Let's go back upstairs," she tells Malorie urgently.

"No!" says Malorie. "We were here first!"

She grabs Polly's hand again and strides forward, dragging Polly behind her. When they reach the group, Polly puts her head down and fixes her eyes to the floor.

Malorie boldly pushes her way through the

grumbling monsters, keeping Polly close behind. They are nearly through the group and out the other side when Polly hears a familiar voice.

"Polly!"

Her heart sinks.

She turns just for a second to look over her shoulder, and there is Buster, waving gleefully at her. "Polly! Hey, Polly! Over here! Hi!"

She glares at him, but Buster doesn't seem to understand.

"Do you *know* that monster?" Malorie says. She sounds horrified.

"No! Of course not!" Polly mumbles.

"He knows your name," Malorie says, looking at Polly curiously.

"I don't know him, OK?" Polly insists. "He lives next door, that's all. He must have heard my mom calling me or something. I don't know!"

She feels anger flare up in her. How dare Buster embarrass her like this in public! She glares at him again.

This time he understands, and Polly sees his face fall.

Oh no! she thinks suddenly. *Not here, Buster. Please don't!*

But even as she watches, she sees Buster begin to change color, and **shrink**. The other monsters stop what they are doing and gather around Buster, watching his strange transformation in confusion.

"Come on!" Polly tells Malorie angrily. "Miss Spinnaker will be waiting."

She hears Buster's voice call out behind her, small and wavering, but she is already striding away, her heart pounding in her chest.

In the bathroom, while Malorie is in a stall, Polly splashes her face with water at the sink. Polly is usually pale, but now she looks white as milk.

"What was *with* that monster?" Malorie calls out from the stall. "Acting like you guys were *friends* or something? Ew. Imagine!"

"I know!" says Polly, a little too loudly.

She closes her eyes and tries to calm her

breathing. That was so close. For the first time ever, Polly feels like she might actually be making a real witch friend. And Buster nearly ruined everything! How dare he? He knows they are meant to ignore each other in public.

Polly feels so angry with him.

"Come on," Malorie says, washing her hands at the sink beside Polly. "Don't worry about it. We'd better get back to the bus or we'll be late."

She puts her hand on Polly's shoulder, and Polly feels a glimmer of happiness creep back into her.

They step out of the bathroom. Polly is moving toward the front entrance when she hears a terrible sound.

It's the sound of monsters teasing and taunting, roaring and jeering. And underneath all that noise is a long, low groaning that wrenches at her heart.

"Buster!" Polly cries.

She can't help it. Buster is hurt! She just knows it. She feels it right in her bones. Polly rushes over and pushes two big monsters to one side to see what is going on.

Buster is curled up on the hard floor in a tiny gray ball.

Polly has never seen him so small and so gray. It's as if every last bit of light has been squeezed out of him, and all that's left is a hard mass of gray fur, twisted and dry as a dishcloth.

All around him, monsters jeer and taunt.

"Look at him!" they laugh, prodding him with their great hairy feet.

"He changes color! He changes color! And look how small he's gotten!"

"Stop it!" Polly yells. "Leave him alone!"

Buster sees Polly, and she watches as he begins to turn a hopeful shade of pale pink.

No, Buster! Polly thinks, but she knows he can't help it.

This color change in Buster only makes the monsters around him more excited. They tease him even louder than before.

"Look at him! Look at Buster changing color when he sees the witch. Buster *loves* the witch. Look at Buster! He's turning *pink!*"

Buster squeezes his eyes shut. A last wheeze escapes from him and he shrinks even more.

"Stop it!" Polly screams. "Stop it! You're hurting him!"

The monsters jeer louder. "The witch loves the monster! The monster loves the witch!"

Their cries are so loud that Polly begins to feel her head **FIZZ.** She shuts her eyes and covers her ears with her hands to try to block out the noise, but the sound in her head just gets louder and louder. Soon it's as if her whole brain is **roaring, loud** as an ocean. **Her skin prickles** and her **blood burns hot.**

Before she can stop herself, her arms fly upward and a shower of sparks shoot from her fingertips.

"STOP!"

she roars, and the sound of
her voice is terrifying.

She feels an electric jolt snap through her. When she opens her eyes, the huddle of monsters has been flung against the far walls of the gallery. They hang there, flattened and panting, eyes goggling in fear.

A shocked silence settles over the gallery.

Polly leans over and pulls Buster to his feet. She hears herself ask if he is OK, before her legs give way beneath her, and the room swirls into black.

Ten

Polly wakes up to the murmuring of Miss Spinnaker's voice above her. She opens her eyes slowly. It takes a moment to work out where she is.

Eventually things swim into focus and she recognizes the ceiling of the school sick room. She has visited here enough to know the long crack above the door that looks like a spider's leg.

Polly often has headaches that take her to the sick room, but nothing like this one.

She slides her eyes slowly to the right, where she can hear Miss Spinnaker's voice and the gentle jangling of her jewelry.

Her brain clenches in pain.

Polly closes her eyes again as her teacher rests a cool palm on her forehead. Some of the pain disappears.

"We've called your mother," Miss Spinnaker says. "She's on her way."

Polly screws her eyes closed even tighter. "My head hurts ..." she murmurs.

"I'm not surprised," Miss Spinnaker says. "That was quite a spell you cast back there."

Images flash into Polly's mind. Sparks flying from her fingertips. Rage boiling through her. The terrified looks on the monsters' faces as they hung from the walls.

Buster, coiled tight and small on the floor.

Polly opens her eyes again. They feel dry and scratchy, as if she has stood too close to a fire.

"I don't know how it happened," Polly whispers. Hot tears leak from her eyes and run down her burning cheeks.

Miss Spinnaker looks at her with concern. Then she glances over her shoulder, leans in, and lowers her voice. "I didn't see what happened. But based on what I saw when I got there, and from reports of those who did see it, you cast an **extraordinary spell** for a witch of your age. Extraordinary."

Polly sees the glimmer of a smile twitch at the corners of Miss Spinnaker's mouth. "And for someone who has trouble making potions? I have to be frank, I am more than a little surprised. Did you know you could do that?"

"No!" Polly says, trying to sit up. A blinding flash of light forces her head back onto the pillow. "No," she says again, more quietly this time. She begins to shake. "Miss Spinnaker, I'm scared," she says. "It was horrible. It was like … it was like there was something *in* me.

Something I couldn't control. I don't ever want to feel that again. Can you take it out of me? I don't want that to happen to me again."

"Polly," Miss Spinnaker says. She turns Polly's face so that she is forced to look directly into her teacher's eyes. "Polly. Listen to me. Yes, I could probably take it out of you, or if not me, the headmistress could. There are spells to remove magic abilities when they aren't being used properly. But why would you want that? What you have is a *gift*. It's an enormous power. Just imagine what you could do with it, once you learn to how to use it properly. I have been teaching at this school for over twenty years and I've never seen such power in a witch as young as you. Imagine, with training, what incredible spells you could do!"

Polly turns away again, and closes her eyes. All she can see is her dear friend Buster, curled up and hurt on the gallery floor.

Where is he now? she wonders. *Is he OK?*

To her surprise, her teacher seems to read her mind. "Your monster friend is OK," she says calmly. "I phoned his school to check up on him."

Polly jerks her eyes open. "He's not my –"

"It's OK, Polly," Miss Spinnaker says very quietly, a small smile on her face. "Not all witches and warlocks think the same way about monsters. I happen to have quite a few close monster friends myself."

Polly's mouth drops open. "Really? But my mom says witches shouldn't mix with monsters."

Miss Spinnaker frowns. "Unfortunately quite a lot of witches feel like that, Polly. Especially those on the Committee, like your mother. Does she know you are friendly with the monster who was being bullied at the gallery?"

Polly nods solemnly. "But I promised her I'd keep it a secret. She will be so upset if other people find out. I think she's worried about what the other moms will say if they know she lets me play with monsters."

"Well, there's no real reason for the other mothers to find out," Miss Spinnaker says, and a curious smile twists her lips. "When I arrived, I rushed over to Malorie to find out what had happened. It will probably come as a surprise to hear, but she remembered the events quite differently."

"Really?" says Polly.

Miss Spinnaker nods. "In her eyes, the spell you did was to protect *her*, not your monster friend. I heard another story from the teacher at Darklands, which I guessed was the true story, as I haven't known you and Malorie to be that close before. And I know that monsters don't usually pick on witches for no reason. But as far as Malorie is concerned, you're her hero! I have no reason to convince anyone otherwise."

"Ha!" Polly laughs weakly. She would laugh louder if her head didn't ache so much. "Me, a hero? That's pretty funny."

Miss Spinnaker takes Polly's hand and smiles at her kindly. "Standing up for a friend *is* being a hero, Polly. No matter who that friend might be. Witch *or* monster."

Her teacher pauses to narrow her eyes at Polly. "Which is why, Miss Oleander Proggett," she continues sternly, using Polly's full name to show just how serious she is, "the headmistress and I have decided not to suspend you from the Academy for using magic out of school grounds *this* time."

Polly fiddles with the thin cotton blanket that has been tucked in around her.

"I didn't mean to," she says glumly. "I got so mad, and then it just … happened."

"I understand," says Miss Spinnaker, her voice softening again. "Oh, look! Here's your mother. Just in time, Mrs. Proggett. Polly has just woken up. I'm sure she'll be very happy to see you."

"**Oh, Polly!**" her mother says, dashing into the room and crouching by Polly's side. "What happened?"

Miss Spinnaker turns to Polly's mother. "Polly was protecting her friend from some unsupervised monsters from Darklands …"

Polly bites down on the smile that is twisting her lips. She is very impressed with the clever way her teacher has told the truth without actually telling the *whole* truth.

"She did quite a spell, Mrs. Proggett! A Protector spell, to be accurate. Quite unlike anything I've seen in a witch so young. Do you have any Black Witches in the family?"

Polly's mother frowns. "Oh, Polly. You poor thing!" Then she turns to answer Miss Spinnaker. "Black Witches? No! Oh, but Polly's father was quite gifted at spells. He worked for the mining company before ..." Her mother's voice drifts off sadly.

"I'm sorry, Mrs. Proggett," Miss Spinnaker says softly. "I had heard that Polly's father was in the accident."

The two of them sit quietly for a moment, remembering all the lives that were lost when the mine collapsed five years ago.

"And Aunt Hilda?" Polly croaks, reminding her mother.

"Oh, yes, that's right. Polly's aunt on her father's side had all the makings of a Black Witch. But she ran away from home at sixteen," Mrs. Proggett sighs. "We don't like to talk about her much. Anyway, no one on my side of the family."

She puts her hand on her daughter's burning forehead.

"Gosh, you were very brave, Polly, to stand up to those monsters," she says, before turning back to Polly's teacher. "You do realize, Miss Spinnaker, that the Committee aren't going to like hearing there were unsupervised monsters at the gallery? Even if they *were* from Darklands. Deidre Halloway has been saying for a long time that monsters are a menace. I must say, after today, I am beginning to agree with her. It's infuriating that the Mayor won't take this threat seriously enough."

"Well, I am sure our Mayor will create new rules as she sees fit," Miss Spinnaker says calmly, "but I don't think monsters mean to cause any harm. Yes, they may be noisy and a little boisterous at times, but we all know there hasn't been a witch harmed by a monster since the uprising of '77. And I don't see signs of that changing any time soon."

"Well, I hope you are right, Miss Spinnaker," says Polly's mother, shaking her head. "I really do hope you are right."

Eleven

Polly sits up in bed with a bowl of lizard broth in her lap, the afternoon sunlight slanting through her window. She takes a couple of obedient spoonfuls while her mother hovers, plumping up pillows and picking up shoes and socks from the floor.

But as soon as her mother leaves the room, Polly puts the bowl down on the carpet where she knows Gumpy will gratefully demolish the oily gray soup.

Polly gazes out the window toward the tree at the end of the backyard. Her stomach churns with worry and lizard broth. She needs to get a message to Buster to see if he is OK. She hasn't been able to stop worrying about him all afternoon.

The image of Buster in the gallery keeps flashing into her mind. The look of hurt and surprise when Polly pretended not to know him.

But this is what we always do! she thinks, trying to forgive herself for her meanness. *He knows that nobody must know we are friends.* A flicker of annoyance at his carelessness sparks through her. *It's not all my fault!*

Polly hears Winifred downstairs, home from school. She is chatting excitedly to their mother in the kitchen, though Polly can't make out what they are saying.

Then Winifred's footsteps bound up the stairs, and her sister bursts into the room.

"Aster at school says you did a **massive** spell at the gallery today! Is that true?"

She swoops over and sits on Polly's bed, her eyes lit with glee. It's rare for Polly to see

Winifred look anything other than bored or annoyed, and she can't help feeling a thrill at her sister's sudden interest in her.

"Everyone's talking about it. What was it like, doing the spell?"

"Well," says Polly, "it just kind of happened. I felt really hot. And there was a flash of light. It was like electricity going through me. It was pretty scary, actually."

She glances at her sister and is pleased to see she's impressed.

"Mom says there were monsters in the gallery. She says they were menacing Malorie Halloway, and you did the spell to scare them off."

"Well, it wasn't *exactly* like that," Polly says.

"Monsters are awful," Winifred shudders. "They're smelly and noisy and they break things and hurt people. I hate them!"

"That's not true," Polly says. "They're not all like that."

Winifred turns to Polly, a cruel smile sliding across her face. "Yes, they are," she says, taunting. "All of them. Mom says. So do all my friends at school."

Polly frowns. She knows exactly where this is going. Winifred is always looking for an opportunity to bring up Buster.

"You used to play with Buster, too," Polly says crossly.

Winifred sneers. "Polly, he's a *monster*. And he's a weird monster at that. You two suit each other. You're both weird."

"Stop being so mean!" Polly says, frowning.

"Stop being so *mean!*" Winifred teases. "It's not my fault you're weird. It's just a fact."

"You're horrible," Polly says, feeling her cheeks stinging pink. "Get out of my room!"

"Why should I?" Winifred says, picking at her flaking nail polish.

"Because it's *my room!*" Polly yells.

"Polly! Winifred!" their mother calls out.

"Mom told me to check up on you," Winifred says, not budging. "I'm just doing what I was told to do."

"**I hate you,**" Polly seethes. "You're the worst sister *ever!*"

But then, as she watches, Polly sees Winifred's face crumple. Her sister bows her head into her hands and begins to make deep sobbing sounds.

"Oh, Winny. I'm sorry!" Polly says, clambering across the bedclothes to reach her sister. "I don't really hate you. I didn't mean it!"

And it's true. When she was little, Polly loved her sister so desperately it hurt. All she really wants is for it to be like that again. When their dad was still alive and everything was right in the world.

She strokes Winifred's glossy black hair. "Winny, I'm sorry. Don't cry!"

Winifred jerks her head out of her hands and grins nastily at Polly. "Ha! Tricked you!" she laughs. "You might not hate me, but I still hate *you!*"

And she jumps up from the bed, laughing loudly at her tremendous joke, and slams Polly's door behind her.

Polly feels her heart **bruised** and heavy.

Twelve

That night, Polly is drifting off to sleep when she hears a rumble at her window. She sits up, her heart racing in her chest like a wild rabbit. The window rattles again.

Then she hears a low, familiar voice.

"Polly?"

"Buster!" Polly gasps, jumping up and pulling back the curtain. "Is that you?"

Sure enough, Buster has pressed his goofy face against the dark glass, already leaving a smear of grease and steam.

Polly doesn't know whether to be thrilled that he is at her window or terrified of them getting caught.

"Buster!" she whispers, pulling open the window. "What are you doing here?"

Buster squeezes through the window and tumbles onto the bed. Polly tries not to notice the trail of twigs and dirt he has left on her clean duvet cover.

"I had to see if you were OK," he says. "When you didn't come to the tree, I got worried. Was I wrong to come?" His face crumples.

"Well, yes, but no," Polly giggles. "Mom would die if she saw you here, but I'm glad you came. I've been worried about you, too."

"Really?" says Buster, grinning widely.

"Of course!" says Polly, wrapping her arms around his big body and sinking her face into his fur. "I'm OK," she says. "Especially now you're here. How about you? I couldn't bear seeing all those monsters teasing you. I just couldn't bear it."

Polly feels Buster shaking. She pulls away to see if he is crying, but Buster is shaking in silent laughter.

"You, a little witch in front of all those great big monsters! You should see how scared they are of me – now they know I've got *you* as a friend! I walk around the playground with my chest out and they say, *Don't mess with Buster. He's got little witch Polly on his side!*"

Polly narrows her eyes. "Hey. You're teasing me!"

Buster wipes a tear of laughter from his eye. "I'm sorry," he says. "It's just that it really is funny thinking about such a small witch doing such a big spell on all those monsters."

"You weren't supposed to let on that we know each other," Polly frowns.

"I know. I'm sorry," Buster grimaces. "I was so happy to see you that I forgot. I couldn't pretend not to be happy to see you. And then I couldn't pretend not to be sad that you ignored me! I messed up. **Big time.** I'm really sorry, Polly."

"Everyone knows about you now, don't they?" Polly says. "At your school?"

Buster nods and shrugs. "The Feelings Monster is what they're calling me. But it's actually not as bad as I thought it would be. In some ways it's easier than pretending to be something I'm not. I've still got you, and the bullies will stop teasing me in a few weeks."

He takes Polly's hand in his big rough one. "But how about you? Are they giving you a hard time for being friends with me?"

Polly smiles. "I don't think anyone knows. Malorie, the witch I was with? She thinks I did the spell to protect *her!*"

"**Oh.**" Buster chews his lip, considering this for a moment. "Aren't you going to tell them the truth?"

Polly cringes. "I don't think so. Do you mind?"

She can see that Buster is disappointed.

"I guess I was hoping we could just tell people now," he says quietly. "It's so tiring having to keep it a secret. I really don't like keeping secrets."

"I know, Buster, but it's worse for a witch to be friends with a monster …" Even as Polly is saying this, she realizes how horrible it sounds. She feels her cheeks burn pink and she looks down at her hands awkwardly.

Buster shrugs. "Whatever you want," he says, and he puts his arm around Polly and pulls her into his side. "I don't mind," he assures her, but Polly notices that his hug isn't quite as tight as usual.

"Thank you, Buster," Polly says, feeling embarrassed. **"You're the best friend ever."**

Suddenly, Buster freezes. His eyes go blank and he stares into the distance.

"Buster? Are you OK?"

But Buster doesn't reply. Without a word, he clambers across the bed and quickly slips out through the window, shutting it behind him.

Polly yanks back the curtain, slides under the sheets and shuts her eyes just as Polly's mother opens the door.

"Polly?" her mother says, standing in the hall light. "Did I hear talking?"

Polly yawns in a way she hopes sounds convincing, but her heart is racing. "Oh, I must have been talking in my sleep."

"Well, that was quite a conversation you were having," her mother says, coming into the room. She sits on the side of Polly's bed and places a cool hand on her forehead. "Oh dear. You're a little feverish! I think you should stay home tomorrow. I'll take the day off work, and you can have a quiet day in bed."

Polly closes her eyes, enjoying her mother's attention.

"**Oh, Polly!**" says her mom, obviously noticing the trail of dirt and leaves on Polly's duvet. "You haven't been letting Gumpy up on your bed, have you? You know she makes a mess."

"Oh, yes. Sorry, Mom," Polly says, relieved. "I won't let her up again."

"Doesn't matter," her mother says, more kindly than usual. "I'll wash your sheets tomorrow."

She gets up and leaves, closing Polly's door softly behind her.

It was nice having her mom sit beside her, like when she was little. Polly considers calling out for her mom to read a bedtime story like she used to, but then decides she'd better check the window instead, in case Buster is still there.

Buster has gone, but written with a clumsy finger in a breath of steam are the words:

See yuo tomoro

Polly smiles and wipes away the message. A warm honey feeling fills her heart when she looks at his crazy spelling, even worse than hers. With Buster in her world, Polly knows she will never truly feel alone.

Thirteen

The next morning, Polly's mother brings her breakfast in bed. She and her sister are **never** allowed to eat in bed because of the crumbs, so Polly knows her mom must be really worried about her to give this kind of attention. "**Hmmmmmm,**" her mother says as she places her palm on Polly's forehead. "You still have a bit of a fever. If you haven't started to pick up by this afternoon, I'll call Doctor Firestone."

Polly **shudders**. Usually the prospect of seeing Doctor Firestone is enough to cure any illness. Last time Polly had to see Doctor Firestone, it took days for the leech marks on her skin to disappear, and the house stunk of boiled herbs for weeks.

Polly looks down at the tray on her lap. **"Chicken eggs,"** she says. "And toast! From wheat bread. Thanks, Mom!"

Polly's mom shrugs and smiles. "I thought you might like a treat. But only because you're sick, OK? Once you're better, it's back to my homemade muesli."

Winifred appears at the door. "How come Polly gets chicken eggs?"

"Your sister is still recovering," their mother says. "So I made her favorite breakfast. If you were unwell I'd do the same for you. Besides, you always say you love my muesli."

Polly has to cover her mouth to hide her smirk.

Winifred scowls. "I do," she mumbles. "It's just that we have it every day."

"Well, when *you're* a working mother with two children, let's hope they're a little more grateful than you are!" their mother huffs, as she stands up and brushes off her skirt. "Don't spill crumbs now, Polly," she says as she leaves.

"Your sheets are already messy from Gumpy."

"I won't," says Polly.

Winifred sticks her tongue out at Polly when their mother's back is turned, but Polly doesn't care. **She has a day at home in bed, and chicken eggs on toast for breakfast!**

Polly tries to read *Little Witches,* the book they are studying at school, but the words swim about on the page even more than usual so she puts it on her bedside table and drifts in and out of sleep.

She is surprised at how tired she feels. Occasionally her mom comes in to take her temperature. Polly wills it to go down each time so she doesn't have to see Doctor Firestone, but when she is still burning up after lunch, her mother makes the call.

"Doctor Firestone is on her way," she says gently, poking her head in through the doorway.

"Oh, Mom!" whimpers Polly. "Did you *have* to?"

But her mom just rolls her eyes and closes the door again.

Polly drifts back to sleep. She wakes to the sound of whispering, and when she opens her eyes, there is Doctor Firestone in all her feathered glory.

Polly sighs.

Doctor Firestone notices Polly is awake and smiles. Her white teeth gleam against her skin.

"**Polly!**" she booms. "You are sick?"

"Yes," says Polly weakly.

"**No matter**! Doctor Firestone will make you better!"

Polly closes her eyes and hopes it will all be over soon.

Firstly, the doctor chants over Polly in a strange language that sounds like grunts mixed with the mooing of a cow. Then she pulls out some tiny crystals from a deep pocket in her feathered cape, and tosses them all over the bed. One of them hits Polly in the face. Polly sighs again. She opens her eyes and brushes a crystal off her cheek.

Doctor Firestone has lit two sticks and is now waving them up and down Polly's body.

Polly coughs a little from the smoke.

"Good!" shouts the doctor. "Good! Cough that sickness out!"

Polly does another cough, fake this time, hoping it will speed up the process.

"Oh, you are sick! You are very sick!" Doctor Firestone says, her eyes rolling white and wild. "I'm afraid I have no choice but to use **Samba!**"

"Samba?" Polly winces.

Doctor Firestone nods. She reaches into yet another deep pocket and pulls out a black and yellow python. It seems to go on and on forever. Polly watches in horror until finally, its head appears, **writhing and hissing**.

"You're going to use that snake on me?" Polly yelps. "What if it bites me?"

"No, oh no!" Doctor Firestone chuckles, like it's the funniest thing she's ever heard. "That's not Samba. That's just a snake. She would most certainly bite you if she could. Then you would be *really* sick! Probably die even!"

She laughs loudly at her own joke, then tosses the snake into a basket and flips the lid down with her bare foot.

Polly notices her long toenails and the silver rings on her toes.

"*This* is Samba!" Doctor Firestone says in an important voice. She reaches even deeper into the same pocket and pulls out a small brown toad. **"Voila!"** she exclaims, holding the toad out on her palm.

Samba croaks obediently.

"A toad?" Polly says.

"Not. Just. A. Toad!" Doctor Firestone bellows, and the glass in Polly's window trembles. "This is a *healing* toad. You will sleep with him on your pillow for one night. Tomorrow I will come back to get him. If he has turned green and his skin is clear, your sickness will be cleared, too. If he is even more warty than he is now, and you also have a face covered in warts, we will have to try something else."

"Er, really?" says Polly. "Do I have to have him on my pillow? I really don't want a face covered in warts. Can we just try something else? I'm actually feeling a bit better already."

"**NO!**" shouts Doctor Firestone. "The toad it is! Doctor Firestone has diagnosed a healing toad, so a healing toad it shall be!"

And with that, she drops the toad onto Polly's pillow, gathers up her feathered robes and baskets, and swishes out the door.

"Oh!" she says, stopping in the doorway and spinning around. "And take two of these every four hours, with water."

She tosses a package of pills onto Polly's bed.

Polly picks up the package and reads the writing on the side. "Headache pills?" she says.

Doctor Firestone shrugs. "In case the toad doesn't work," she says, and then, with another **SWOOP** of her cape, she is out the door.

As soon as she's out of sight, Polly pulls out a tissue from the box by her bed, scoops up the slimy toad, and drops it into her bedside drawer.

"Sorry, Samba," Polly says, her mouth curling in disgust, "but you are *not* sleeping on my pillow. There's no way I want to risk waking up with warts all over my face. I have enough problems as it is!"

Samba blinks twice in reply.

Fourteen

Whether it's the headache pills or the toad in her drawer, Polly's fever has subsided by the time her mother checks up on her later that afternoon.

"Thank goodness for Doctor Firestone," she mutters, plumping up Polly's pillows.

Polly says nothing.

"Now, there's a visitor for you downstairs," her mom says, smiling. "Do you feel up to it?"

"A visitor?" Polly says.

Surely Buster wouldn't come to the front door? But she knows if Buster had turned up at their door, Polly would have heard about it from up here.

"Who is it?" she asks nervously.

"Malorie Halloway. That's nice, isn't it? I'm so pleased you're starting to make friends at school," she says.

"Malorie?" Polly says, her heart beginning to leap about in her chest.

Polly has never had a school friend over before. She skims the room with fresh eyes to check there is nothing babyish or uncool on display that might embarrass her. When her mother leaves the room to fetch Malorie, Polly quickly shoves a raggedy old doll and a fluffy black toy cat under her bed.

Then she checks her reflection in the dressing table mirror, drags a brush through her hair and hops back into bed just as her mother and Malorie appear in the doorway.

"Well," her mother says, smiling more broadly than Polly has seen her smile in years, "I'll leave you two little witches alone then. Malorie, send my regards to your mother, won't you? Though I expect I'll be seeing her at our next Committee meeting."

"Thanks, Mom," Polly says, awkwardly patting down the duvet over her legs.

"Shall I bring you up some nettle tea and beetle biscuits?" Polly's mother asks, hovering in the doorway.

"No, thank you, Mrs. Proggett," Malorie says politely. "I don't eat anything after school. I might spoil my dinner."

"Oh, of course!" Polly's mother says, and Polly hears her muttering to herself as she drifts into the hallway. "Such lovely manners!"

As soon as Polly's mom has closed the door, Malorie dashes over to Polly's bed and pulls out a newspaper from her schoolbag.

"Have you seen the papers, Polly?" she giggles. *"We're famous!"*

"Oh!" Polly says, taken aback. This is the

last thing she was expecting to hear. "Um, no."

Malorie flattens the newspaper across Polly's knees, and turns to the second page.

"Look!" she says.

Polly picks up the paper with trembling hands. The first thing she sees, at the top of the page, is a big black-and-white image of her face, cropped out of last year's class photo. It was the year she was missing a tooth and had cut her hair short, but it's unmistakably her.

There's a smaller photo below of Malorie, sitting on a big floral couch in a very pretty living room. When Polly looks closer she sees Malorie has curled her hair and could quite possibly even be wearing lipstick.

Lipstick? Polly thinks.

Then her eyes flick to the heading:

YOUNG WITCH SAVES FRIEND

Polly's heart begins to pound. She looks up at Malorie.

"You're a hero, Polly!" Malorie says, tapping the newspaper to encourage Polly to keep reading.

Polly looks back down at the article and begins to read slowly, her finger tracing the words.

An innocent school field trip went horribly wrong when a group of young students from Miss Madden's Academy of Witchcraft and Spells, an elite school for witches and warlocks, was visiting the National Gallery yesterday. Believing themselves to be the only students at the gallery that day, they were horrified to discover that a group of obnoxious monsters from Darklands School for Monsters had turned up soon after they arrived.

"We knew they were going to cause trouble," young Malorie Halloway, a Grade Five witch from Miss Madden's Academy, explains. "As soon as they got off the bus they were yelling at us and calling us names."

"But that's not true," Polly says, looking up at Malorie.

Malorie shrugs. "Just keep reading!"

Poor Malorie, still in shock after the terrible incident, goes on: "Our teacher did what she could to keep us away from the monsters, but my best friend, Polly Proggett, and I had to go to the bathroom. The ones upstairs were already full so we went downstairs. That's when we saw the monsters. They were acting wild and crazy and they didn't have a teacher with them. I was scared they were going to hurt us. I wanted to run away, but then they saw us and started coming for us. That's when Polly did the spell."

"The Spell," as everyone is now calling it, consisted of blasting thirteen almost fully grown monsters against the far walls of the gallery, allowing Polly and Malorie to escape unharmed.

Professor Freidreich, a leading spell expert from the University of Printania, explains the unlikelihood of such a young and inexperienced witch having these capabilities.

"It's most uncommon," he says. "Spells of this magnitude usually take many years of training to master. Occasionally, a high degree of emotion can trigger such a force – such as a mother rescuing her baby from danger. This is the only explanation that seems reasonable. I can merely speculate on the depth of friendship between these two witches for such a powerful protector spell to have been triggered in the young witch. It's quite a feat, really. Quite remarkable."

While this may well be a heroic feat from young Polly Proggett, Malorie's mother, Mrs. Deidre Halloway, provides us with some more sobering thoughts to end on: "It's not right," she says from her living room in New Hanwood, "that the government allows monsters to mix freely with our witches and warlocks. It must be stopped. This was a near crisis that was luckily averted by some quick work on Polly's part. But what if she hadn't been there beside my young Malorie? Who knows what those monsters would have done to my daughter! Or any of the young witches or warlocks at the gallery, for that matter. It's terrifying to even think about.

"I believe this is all the proof we need that it's well and truly time to crack down on monsters. They are a menace to our society. And I'm not the only one who thinks so."

Do you agree with Mrs. Halloway's opinion? Phone in to the *Warlock Times* and we will publish your thoughts on the Monster Dilemma tomorrow.

Polly looks up slowly. Her head is spinning.

Is that really what Malorie thinks happened?

But even as she's thinking this, Malorie leans over to give Polly a massive hug.

"Thank goodness for you, Polly! You're my *best* friend," she sighs.

Despite her confusion, Polly's heart soars. *Best friend?* Did she really hear that right? Polly can't contain the huge smile that stretches across her face. Polly has never had a witch as a best friend before.

"I brought you a present," Malorie says. "To thank you for everything you did for me. It's not much but …" As she is talking, she reaches into the pocket of her school uniform.

Polly gasps when she sees what Malorie is giving her. "Your mood pen? No, I can't take that!"

Malorie's mood pen is *famous*. It's the newest thing in stationery, but Malorie is the only witch with parents rich enough – and indulgent enough – to buy one for her. A mood pen's ink changes color, depending on what mood you are in.

As Polly tests it out on the edge of the newspaper, it changes from **sparkly pink** to **purple,** then **lilac**.

"That means you're happy," Malorie says, grinning. "Which I think means you should absolutely take it."

"Oh, wow! Really?" Polly says. "I mean, are you sure …?"

Polly feels like the right thing to do would be to hand it back to Malorie. It was, after all, a very expensive gift from her parents. But watching the ink change color as she doodles over the newspaper, she finds she can't quite let it go.

And for a moment, Polly feels so happy it's as if her chest might burst. A new best friend and a mood pen! She can't imagine how life could be any more perfect.

"Of course you should have it, Polly," Malorie says. "Gosh, it's nothing compared to what you did for me yesterday. You're a hero! Everyone says so. We all missed you at school today!"

"Really?" Polly says. "We?"

"Of course!" Malorie says. "Everyone's dying to see you – now that you're a hero! I was the only one allowed to come and visit you, though. You know, seeing as I'm your best friend."

"Thank you!" Polly mumbles.

It's so hard for her to believe this is all real. It feels like a dream. A very strange dream indeed. Only the day before, Polly had no friends at school. And now everyone wants to know her.

This is what it must feel like to be popular, she thinks. She decides she likes the feeling very much.

"Oh! I haven't even asked how you are," Malorie says.

"Better." Polly shrugs, then smiles. "Thanks to him."

She opens her bedside drawer a crack for Malorie to peer inside.

"Ew! Is that a toad?" Malorie grimaces. "You didn't have Doctor Firestone over, did you?" Malorie claps her hand over her mouth.

Polly laughs, nodding wildly.

"Did she do the smoke thing?"

Polly nods again, laughing even harder.

"And the crystals?"

"Yes!" Polly squeals. "And the chanting!"

"Oh no! Not the chanting? The one that sounds like a grunt ..."

"Mixed with a cow mooing!"

"Yes!"

The two witches roll around on the bed, snorting hysterically. Polly's stomach hurts from laughing.

But then suddenly, mid-laughter, Malorie stops and sits up. She puts her finger on her lips, eyes wide.

"Shhh!" she says. "Did you hear that?"

Polly listens. There is a rattling at her window. Her stomach sinks.

"I can't hear anything," she lies.

"Listen! There's definitely something there," Malorie says. "Open the curtains!"

"It's nothing!" Polly insists. "Just the tree outside my window. It bangs against the glass sometimes."

Then they hear a low, gentle calling.

"*Polleeeee. Po-lleeeeee* ..."

"That. Is. Not. A. Tree," Malorie says slowly.

Polly sighs and crawls over to the window. She pulls the curtain open a crack, but Malorie is right behind her.

Buster's big hairy face is pressed to the window.

"Is that a ... monster?" Malorie says in disgust. "What's he doing here?"

"He just lives next door," Polly says. "I can't help it if he keeps coming around."

She feels **angry** at Buster for humiliating her like this. For spoiling this moment. She never asked him to come around!

"Go away!" she shouts. She yanks the curtain closed.

"Oh, how awful!" Malorie says. "Was that the monster from the gallery? The one that was waving at you? Have you told your mother he just turns up at your window like that?"

"**No!**" says Polly quickly. "No. It's not like that. He's not dangerous or anything. He doesn't mean any harm. He just ... hangs around a bit."

Her voice peters out. She looks up at Malorie, wondering how much she can tell her.

"We used to ... play together. When we were little. His family's quite nice, really," she ventures. "His mom is kind. She looks after other monsters. The ones that no one else wants."

She is almost pleading now. Hoping that Malorie will see things a little differently, hoping she will see Polly's point of view.

But Malorie's expression grows stony. Her pretty top lip curls into a sneer, and she tosses her plaits over her shoulders.

"Polly, I don't think I can be best friends with someone who mixes with monsters," she says coldly. "Imagine what the witches at school would say."

Polly panics. She feels Malorie's interest in her slipping away with every second, and with it, any chance of being popular. "Don't tell anyone, Malorie. Please don't. I won't play with him again. I promise."

Malorie looks at Polly, unblinking. "Promise?" she says.

"Yes, I promise," Polly pleads. "I don't like monsters either!" she says, a little too forcefully. "In fact, I **hate** them!"

A slow smile moves across Malorie's face.

"All right," she says. "Then I suppose we can still be best friends." She stands up and brushes down her skirt. "I'll see you tomorrow at school then?" she says briskly, and before Polly can entice her to stay a little longer, Malorie is out the door.

Polly sits back on her bed, deflated. Then she hears a shuffling at her window and a gentle cracking of branches.

Oh no! she thinks. *Was Buster listening?*

She rushes to open the curtain to try and explain.

There, on her windowsill, is a bedraggled posy of flowers, damp and wilted from the heat of Buster's paws.

Fifteen

"She's here!" Rosemary yells at the top of her voice.

She runs up to give Polly a **huge hug**. Polly stands awkwardly in Rosemary's arms. She has only been in the playground a moment, and already she is surrounded by excitable witches.

"Willow! Malorie!" calls Rosemary. "Polly's here!"

Malorie runs up to them, and Rosemary lets go of Polly to let Malorie in. After all, Malorie is Polly's *best* friend.

"I'm so glad you're better!" Malorie says. "We didn't know how long you'd be away from school."

"That's right," Willow agrees. "We had to start the club without you. But now you're here, you can be in charge."

"What club?" Polly asks.

Malorie smiles. "Witches Against Monsters."

Polly's head starts to buzz a little. "I don't know that game," she says.

Malorie snorts. "It's not a *game*, Polly," she says slowly, like Polly isn't very smart. "It's a *movement*.

Haven't you heard? Our newspaper article received heaps of calls from witches who are sick of monsters hanging around our streets. They are horrible. Noisy and smelly and even dangerous. Mom has always said so, and now other witches and warlocks are agreeing. Look! Mom even made us badges to wear."

Malorie points to a small round badge on the lapel of her school blazer with a black *W* printed on it.

Polly looks at the witches huddled around her. They are all wearing the same badge, and before Polly has a chance to protest, Malorie is pinning one onto her uniform, too.

"That's *W* for witch," Malorie says as she's pinning. "You need to make it clear whose side you're on. Some witches are still in support of monsters, but this shows you're with us."

"Um, I don't know if I really want to wear this," Polly says anxiously. She loves the thought of being in a club, but she is not sure *this* is the kind of club she wants to be a part of.

Malorie narrows her eyes. "But if you don't wear it, how will people know you're not a friend of monsters? *Are* you a friend of monsters?"

Polly feels her cheeks heat up. She looks at Willow and Rosemary, and sees them watching her closely. Her mouth opens but nothing comes out.

Willow's face falls. "Oh. You're not a friend of monsters, are you? Polly?" She takes a step back.

Rosemary steps back, too. "My mother told me I wasn't to talk to friends of monsters," she says nervously.

"No, no, of course not!" Polly says, finally finding her voice. "I just don't think they're dangerous, that's all. They might be noisy and sometimes even a bit smelly, but they're not dangerous."

"Yes, they *are*," Malorie corrects her. "They attacked us in the gallery! If it wasn't for you, I might not be standing here today." She turns to the other witches. "She doesn't remember it very clearly," she explains. "When she passed out, her brain got all **muddled**. And she's been sick, too. Isn't that right, Polly?"

Polly chews her lip. "I don't know," she mumbles, and she really doesn't know anymore. She doesn't know what she thinks. She doesn't know what she remembers. It all feels so long ago now, and she *has* been unwell.

The bell rings.

"Come on, let's go!" Malorie says cheerily. "Or we'll be late for class."

She grabs Polly's hand and steers her through the playground. Along the way, Malorie waves at the witches and warlocks who are staring at them. Some of them hold up three fingers in the sign of a *W.*

Malorie and the other witches hold up three fingers in return.

Polly is not sure about everyone suddenly looking at them like they are famous, but Malorie seems to be loving it.

As they head into the classroom, Polly looks around for Miss Spinnaker. She will know what Polly should do.

But Miss Spinnaker is not there.

At the front desk is old Mrs. Crabbe, their

substitute teacher, scowling at the witches as they drift in.

"Well, if it's not our local hero," she says to Polly, screwing her face into an almost smile. "The Defeater of Monsters. You've caused quite a sensation this week, haven't you?"

"Miss Spinnaker isn't here today," Malorie tells Polly as they walk down the long aisle to the back of the class. She is still holding tightly to Polly's hand.

"Where is she?" Polly asks, her voice rising into a squeak. She looks toward Valentine, who has a worried expression on her face.

Valentine whispers, "Maybe she's sick?"

Polly feels a chill pass through her as she

looks down at her desk. Someone has placed a newspaper there. This time, there is a photo of Polly on the front page. A more recent one this time. And the headline:

LOCAL WITCH'S HEROICS TRIGGER LONG-AWAITED WITCHES AGAINST MONSTERS MOVEMENT

"*See?*" hisses Malorie. "You're famous! Exciting, isn't it?"

Polly folds the paper in half and places it in her desk. Then she looks toward the board, breathing slowly to calm herself.

Sixteen

When the bell rings for recess, Malorie grabs Polly's hand again and pulls her outside into the sunshine. The other witches follow them. They make their way to the bench underneath the old lallypod tree, with its brilliant show of autumn leaves.

There are already two witches sitting there from another class, and they wave excitedly when they see Polly.

"Polly! Polly! Sit with us!" Gretel and Capsum call, and Polly feels her chest fill with pleasure.

All around the playground, when witches and warlocks see Polly, they point and smile and wave. Even though she still has a not-quite-right feeling at the pit of her stomach, Polly is beginning to enjoy all the attention. Only a couple of days ago, no one wanted to sit next to her. Now she feels like a *star!*

"What do you have for lunch?" Malorie asks, peering into Polly's tidy plastic lunch box. It's divided into neat little compartments. Polly peels off the lid of one of the smaller plastic containers nestled inside and wrinkles up her nose.

"Bats' ears," Polly sighs, holding up a crispy brown triangle.

"Swap?" Malorie asks, holding up a beancake. "I love bats' ears. Especially the salted ones."

"Sure!" says Polly. She takes the beancake gladly, and sinks her teeth into the sweet, powdery pastry. "Thanks! We hardly ever have beancakes. Mom only gives us healthy food."

"My mom's the same," Capsum says sympathetically.

"**Oh!**" Rosemary says, suddenly noticing Malorie's pen pointing out of Polly's top pocket. "You've got a mood pen, too! I'm *so* jealous."

Malorie grins and grabs Polly's hand. "No, it's mine. I gave it to Polly to thank her for saving my life in the gallery."

"Oh, you're so lucky," Rosemary and Willow say, their voices twisting slightly with jealousy.

And right then Polly *does* feel lucky. Perhaps she's the luckiest witch in the world. Malorie is the most popular witch in class, and she has chosen Polly to be her best friend.

Polly has felt lonely at school for so long that she decides she's going to enjoy this new feeling.

She loves Buster to bursting, but Polly needs witch friends, too.

At that moment, three cute warlocks from the class above them wander past. Markus, whom all the witches in Polly's class have a crush on, tilts his chin in Polly's direction and raises his eyebrows in a solemn hello.

"Pretty smackin' spell you did the other day," he says, and the other warlocks nod in agreement. "What's your name again?"

Willow jabs Polly in the ribs and Polly's voice comes out in an annoying squeak. "Um, Polly!" she says, then clears her throat.

"Polly," repeats Markus approvingly, and then he and his friends keep walking.

As soon as they are out of hearing range, the witches squeal in excitement.

"Oh my jiddering sorcery!" Willow gasps. "Markus said hello to you, Polly. Markus!"

"You are so totally a hero in school right now," Gretel sighs.

"How about those monsters?" Rosemary says. "So scary, right?"

Polly takes another bite of the beancake and slides her eyes across to Malorie. She has been loving the attention up until this moment, but now that the conversation has again turned to what happened in the gallery she begins to feel sticky with discomfort.

"I know!" says Malorie. "We were so scared,

weren't we, Polly? I didn't know what they might do."

Polly chews slowly. The beancake catches in her throat.

"But you were amazing, Polly!" Gretel says, slapping Polly on the shoulder. "Incredible! I wish I'd seen that spell you did."

"Me too," Capsum agrees.

"We had no idea you could do spells like that," says Rosemary in awe.

Malorie puts her hand on Polly's knee, nodding somberly. "I don't know what I would have done if you hadn't been there to protect me." She looks straight into Polly's eyes as she says this.

Polly stares back, like she's trying to read a message there.

But then Malorie tosses her plaits back over her shoulders and turns to the other witches. "And how cool is it that I got into the paper?"

"So cool!" Gretel says. "You looked so pretty in that photo. Were you wearing lipstick?"

Malorie smiles and shrugs. "Maybe?"

"Were you scared?" Willow asks Polly.

Polly looks down at the half-eaten beancake in her hand. She doesn't feel very hungry anymore.

"I don't really feel like talking about it, if that's OK?" she mumbles.

She just wishes everyone would stop talking about what happened at the gallery.

"Come on, guys," Malorie says, putting her arm around Polly's shoulder. "It was a pretty scary time. I'm not surprised Polly doesn't want to talk about it."

"I know. Let's play witches versus monsters!" Rosemary says, dropping her half-chewed trotter into her lunchbox.

"Um … how do you play?" Polly asks, relieved the moment has passed.

"It's easy," Malorie says. "The one who is the monster has a scarf tied over their eyes so they can't see. Everyone else runs around them in a circle and tries to tap them with their hand.

If the monster catches one of them, then they become a witch and the one who's caught becomes a monster. Get it?"

Polly nods. Gretel is first up as the monster. The witches run around her in a circle, getting faster and faster.

"**Monster!**" they call out, as they dart their hands in to tap Gretel. "**Monster! Monster! Big, ugly monster!**"

Gretel swings her arms around wildly, giggling each time she nearly catches a witch before they slip away.

Polly finds herself laughing in the excitement of it all. She dips in and out between the other witches, occasionally colliding with one of them and snorting with laughter, narrowly missing Gretel's swinging hands.

Finally, Gretel catches Rosemary around the wrist.

"Caught!" she yells, yanking the scarf off.

Rosemary takes her place. Willow is caught next, then Capsum, then Malorie. Polly is more cautious than the others and so has avoided being caught up until now, but Malorie seems determined that it be her turn next. At the precise moment Polly ducks her hand in toward Malorie, Malorie catches it swiftly and cleanly, like she has been waiting only for this.

"Your turn," she says, smiling, and hands the scarf over to Polly.

Polly thinks she glimpses a tiny flicker of menace in Malorie's smile, but then it's gone. Malorie ties the scarf tightly around Polly's eyes, and the witches circle around her.

"**Monster**," they begin to call, gently at first, then louder and louder. "**Monster! Monster! Big, ugly monster!**" They step in to jab her in the ribs, her shoulders, her back.

Polly swings her hands around in the darkness but touches nobody. The witches circle closer. Polly can feel the warmth of their bodies swishing past. She swings her arms about but the jeering is coming from all sides and makes her head swim.

She steps forward and gets a jab in the back.

She spins around and
receives another
jab on her arm.

Even though she knows it's only a game, Polly begins to feel panic swelling in her chest. The witches' voices sound louder and louder in her ears, and the jabbing seems to get harder and harder.

"Monster, monster!" She hears Malorie's voice close to her ear. "Big, ugly, hairy monster," she hisses. "You can't get me."

Polly's head begins to fizz. She doesn't like this game anymore. She reaches for the scarf over her eyes, but someone pulls her hand away.

"You're not free yet!" Malorie says in her ear. "You have to catch someone first!"

Polly feels her breathing get faster. Her heart is pounding. Finally, the bell rings and the whirlpool of witches around her scatters.

Polly jerks the scarf down from her eyes and sees Rosemary, Willow, Capsum and Gretel running back to the tree to collect their lunch boxes.

Polly stands there, breathing hard, her head spinning. She looks up at Malorie, who is smiling.

"Coming?" she says sweetly.

Seventeen

*A*ll around Polly, witches and warlocks are making their way back to class.

As Polly's head clears, she looks at Malorie. Even though Malorie is smiling and holding her hand out toward her, Polly sees, quite clearly, that Malorie is not her friend.

Not really. Not a **true** friend.

Buster is her friend. Buster, who is kind and lovely and likes Polly no matter what. True friends don't care two hoots about magical pens, or being famous or popular. And they would never make you pretend to be someone you're not.

Polly suddenly has the sinking feeling that by choosing Malorie, she has broken her very best friend's great big heart in two.

Her hands shaking, Polly slowly unpins the badge on her chest. She knows Malorie is watching as she turns the badge upside down and pins it back on her uniform.

The *W* is now an *M*.

"What are you doing?" Malorie says, her mouth dropping open in horror.

"I'm a friend of monsters," Polly says, sounding calmer than she feels. "And if that's not OK with you, I'm afraid we can't be friends."

She takes Malorie's beautiful mood pen out of her pocket and holds it out.

"What are you talking about?" Malorie hisses, her eyes flitting from side to side.

Students are stopping on their way back to class to watch this small spectacle.

"Monsters are bad. They are noisy and smelly and they hurt witches," insists Malorie.

"**No,**" Polly says. "There are bad monsters and there are good monsters. Just like witches and warlocks. They are just different than us, that's all! And you should never treat anyone badly just because they aren't like you. That's. Not. Fair. And those monsters in the gallery never meant to hurt us, and you know it. You know the truth, Malorie. You're just pretending that you don't."

"You're mad, Polly," Malorie says, backing away and shaking her head. "You're completely mad. I tried to help you. I thought you would be *grateful!*" she spits. "You could have been the most popular witch in school. But now – you know what? *No one* will like you. No one will *ever* want to be your friend!"

She throws up her hands. "Good luck being all alone again, Polly!" she yells, as she runs off through the small crowd that has gathered.

Polly watches her go and takes a deep breath to steady herself. Then, shoving her hands in her pockets to hide the shaking, she slowly walks back to class.

A witch **bumps** into her. Polly keeps walking. The witch **bumps** into her again.

"Hey!" says Polly. "Careful!"

But when she turns to look at the witch who is hovering nearby – a witch from another grade level whose name Polly doesn't even know – she notices a curious thing.

The witch's hand is hanging by her side in a most unnatural way. Her thumb and little finger are curled up into her palm and her three middle fingers are pointing to the ground.

Polly gasps. *Is that an* M?

Polly glances up at the witch's face. She winks at Polly before she jogs off and is lost in the crowd. Polly blinks.

Another warlock walks past. He widens his eyes at Polly, ever so slightly. Polly looks down at his hand. Like the witch, he too is pointing three fingers down to the ground.

Polly can't believe it. As she moves through the jumble of students making their way back to class, she spots more and more witches and warlocks catching her eye, and when she looks down at their hands they are all making the sign of an *M*.

M for monster.

Polly can't hold back the smile. *You are wrong, Malorie Halloway*, she thinks. *I am not alone. I am not alone at all!*

Eighteen

Polly runs all the way home from the bus stop, dumps her bag in the kitchen and runs outside to the tree. She scrambles up the wide knotted trunk, her toes finding their way into the familiar holes, and within moments she has reached the branches which stretch out like open arms. This is the place that has sheltered Polly and Buster's precious friendship from the world for so long.

It has only been a few days since she was last here with Buster, but so much has happened since then. She can't wait to tell Buster how she stood up to Malorie Halloway once and for all.

Polly tips back her head and cups her hands around her mouth.

"Awrooooo! Awroooooooooo!"

she calls, and then leans back against the trunk to wait for him.

But Buster doesn't come.

Polly calls again and again. But it doesn't take her long to know, deep in the very bottomest part of her belly, that even if Buster can hear her, he isn't coming to the tree this afternoon. Maybe not tomorrow, or the next day either.

Maybe he'll never come again?

He is too hurt and too sad, and she is the one who has made him feel like that. She feels silly to think he would have forgiven her so easily. Polly slides back down the tree trunk, rushes down their front walk and through the gates to the house next door.

Buster's mom answers the door. "I'm sorry, love," she says kindly. "He's just not feeling himself at the moment. Give him a couple of days, all right? He'll be back to his old cheery self by then."

"Can you please tell him that I came?" Polly asks, her tummy squirming with worry.

"Of course, *pippikin*. If you want, you can try calling around again tonight after dinner. Bruce and I will be at the meeting, and Buster will be on his own. He might like the company."

"Meeting?" Polly asks.

"Oh yes. At the Town Hall. I imagine your ma will be there too?" Patsy says. "The Committee has called a meeting with the Mayor." She rolls her eyes. "That Mrs. Halloway and her crowd really do have a spider in their underwear about us monsters. If everybody just minded their own business, we'd all get along fine."

Polly feels her cheeks heat up. "It's all my

fault," she says, her head hanging down. "Because of that spell I did in the gallery."

Patsy lifts Polly's chin with her big hairy paw. "You did a good thing for a friend, Polly. You stood up for Buster when his classmates were bullying him – we know that. But witches and monsters choose to believe what they want to. Don't you worry your pretty little head about a thing, my *lovekin*. It's all just a fizzle in a cauldron. It will blow over soon, I'm sure."

Polly nods hopefully. Then she trudges back down the bumpy path, through the wild and overgrown backyard to her own home.

Winifred is waiting for her.

"Where have *you* been?" she asks.

She is sitting on the front doorstep, twisting her long black ponytail around her fingers and chewing on an aniseed root.

"Nowhere," Polly mutters.

"I bet you've been at Buster's house," Winifred says. "You're just lucky I don't tell Mom."

"Tell her what you want," Polly says.

She is tired of all this secrecy now. Buster is right. A friend is a friend. You should stand up for them no matter what. Polly only wishes she had done this before. Now maybe Buster will never want to be her friend again.

How could she have possibly chosen mean Malorie Halloway over dear, kind Buster? Polly feels awful.

She tries to pass Winifred, but her sister blocks the way.

"Mom!" Polly calls.

"Mom's out," Winifred says. "I'm in charge."

"Where is she?" Polly frowns.

"Committee meeting," says Winifred. "She's left us some tripe and pine-needle stew. I ate the rest of the toast." She grins.

"**Winifred!**" Polly says. "Mom bought that for *me*."

Winifred shrugs. "You're too spoiled anyway."

Polly pushes past her sister and runs upstairs to her room. She slams her door loudly so that Winifred gets the message. Then she flumps down onto her bed. She can hear Gumpy sniffing hopefully at the door, but she doesn't get up to let her in.

Polly sighs and looks up at the star stickers she pasted to her ceiling all those years ago. It's not dark enough for them to glow properly, but they feel comforting all the same. She remembers her dad lifting her onto his shoulders and walking her around the room so she could stick them on the ceiling, one by one.

"They're magic stars," he had whispered to her. "You can't see them during the day, but they shine at night. Just like real stars. If you ever wake up in the night and feel scared, you just have to look up at those stars and know that I am close by. Always."

A hot tear slithers down her cheek. "No, you're not," she says angrily to the stars.

She gazes up at the ceiling as if the stars might answer her, even though she is old enough to know there is nothing *magic* about glow-in-the-dark stickers. Polly knows it's silly to feel angry at her dad for dying, but she can't help it. If he was here, she is sure everything would be different.

Polly reaches over to her bedside table and pulls a carved wooden box out of the top drawer. Then she slides her fingers under the ledge of the table and pulls a small gold key out of the join. She unlocks the box and opens the lid. There's a jumble of colored feathers and shells and smooth pebbles that Buster has given her over the years. But at the back of the box lies the little purple silk pouch stitched with gold stars. It's the only thing she still has of her father's.

After he died, Polly's mother had given the pouch of stones to Polly, even though Winifred had wanted them for herself.

"He always said that if anything ever happened to him, this pouch should go to Polly," their mother had explained to Winifred.

Polly picks it up, undoes the drawstring and tips the contents onto her palm. Three smooth gemstones topple out, one blue as the sky, one pink as blush and one a clear and gold-hued amber. The blue one has three linked circles carved into it, and the pink one has three painted white stripes, but it is the amber one that is by far the most intriguing.

Polly holds it up to the light and peers inside. Embedded into the stone is another smaller stone shaped like an eye with a black center. Sometimes, when she moves it slowly, it looks as if the eye is watching her, but Polly knows this is just a trick of the light. Polly drops the stones back into their pouch, and slips the pouch into her pocket.

This is as close as she will ever get to her father now.

Nineteen

The light softens into pink and Polly watches the shadows of the leaves quivering on her walls. Once she knows it's late enough, she jumps out of bed and shoves her desk chair up underneath the door handle. She's not sure it will keep her sister out completely, but it will slow her down. Then she opens her window and climbs out onto the sill. She is a good tree climber but all the same, when she looks down at the drop below, her heart leaps up into her mouth.

Taking a deep breath, she lowers herself onto the only branch she can reach. It is too weak for her weight and it cracks immediately, dropping Polly through the air until she hits another branch, which catches her. Polly clings on, breathing heavily and rubbing at the long scratch on her arm that's beading with blood. She spits onto her hand and rubs it along the graze, but it only stings even more.

Polly hisses under her breath, then inches down the long branch toward the trunk of the tree. From here she feels confident enough to clamber down between the branches, until she is finally low enough to jump to the ground. Just as her feet hit the earth, the back door swings open and Winifred is there, framed in light.

"Polly!" she calls out. "There you are!"

Polly's first instinct is to run, but there is something strange about the look on Winifred's face that makes her hesitate.

"Polly, wait!" she says. "Stop! Buster's in trouble."

Polly narrows her eyes. She is used to her sister's nasty tricks. "I don't believe you," she says, but the jumping frogs in her tummy are telling her otherwise.

"It's true," Winifred says, grabbing Polly's sleeve, her eyes wide and serious. "Just listen to me. I was talking to Tabitha on the phone just now, and she told me the meeting went really badly. Her mom said that the Committee witches are out of control. That horrible Mrs. Halloway has been saying things about Buster. She says Malorie says Buster comes to your window *all* the time. That he's planning to hurt you. She says it was Buster who was going to attack Malorie at the gallery. The Mayor refused to believe her, so Mrs. Halloway stormed out of the meeting in a rage. That's when Tabitha's mom left too. But now Mrs. Halloway is leading a group of witches, and they are on their way to Buster's house. You have to warn him, Polly. Get him somewhere safe until his parents get home."

Polly stares at her sister. "You don't even *like* Buster! Why would you want to protect him?"

"Look, I might not be his friend but I don't want him to get *hurt*," Winifred says. "I'm not *that* horrible!"

Polly can see a glimpse of the sister Winifred used to be. The one who was kind and truthful. The one who played with her and Buster when they were young. And she knows with all her heart that Winifred is telling the truth.

"Hurry, Polly!" she pleads, pushing Polly out into the night. "Go! I'll cover for you when Mom gets home."

Polly spins around and races down the side path. From the front gate she sees the horde of witches storming down the street toward them, Malorie Halloway's mother in front, her silver-streaked hair whipping about in the wind and her long red nails clutching her cape at her throat.

She spots Polly and shrieks. Polly runs faster than she ever has, up Buster's front walk and toward his tall wooden door.

"Buster!" she yells, slamming the door with her fists. "Buster! Open up!" She can see the light on at his bedroom window. "Buster!" she shouts. "I know you're mad at me, but you have to let me in. You're in trouble!"

Polly races along the side of the house. She

tries the back door, but it is locked. Next to it is a small, dark window. Polly pushes at the dusty window and, to her surprise, it shifts a little. She pushes harder and it slowly creaks upward. She hoists herself up onto the sill and squeezes through the narrow space until she tumbles onto the floorboards on the other side.

"Ow!" she cries.

She stands up, rubbing her knee and waiting for her eyes to adjust to the dark. Sliding her hand along the wall, she inches toward a crack of light that she hopes will lead into the main part of the house. She has no idea whose room she has tumbled into until she hears a low growl.

Maggie.

She turns around slowly and sees Maggie's eyes glinting in the dark. Polly's heart starts to pound.

"It's OK, Maggie," Polly says, as calmly as she can, "it's just me, Polly. Buster's friend. I was over the other night, remember?"

Maggie growls again. In the distance, Polly can hear the noise of the witches approaching the house, shrieking and cackling.

"It's OK, Maggie," Polly says, inching forward.

She is desperate to find Buster, and time is

running out. Maggie shuffles up behind her and sniffs her neck. Polly can feel her breath on her skin and smell the stink of her oily hair.

"It's OK, Maggie," Polly repeats nervously, patting Maggie's scaly arm. "It's OK."

She reaches the door and slowly opens it, letting the hall light spill into Maggie's room. Maggie cowers in the light and her eyes are so large and so fearful that Polly understands why Buster's mother feels the need to protect her.

Suddenly there is a pounding at the front door. Maggie jumps in fright and pushes past Polly and out into the hallway.

"No, Maggie!" Polly yells, and grabs Maggie's arm to pull her back into the safety of her room.

Maggie wheels around and sinks her teeth into Polly's hand. Then she scuttles down the hallway and into the laundry room, where it is dark.

Polly clutches her hand to her chest. She can barely breathe for the pain.

The banging comes again. "Open up, Polly Proggett!" comes Mrs. Halloway's shrill voice. "We know you're in there!"

Polly takes in big gulps of air to try to ease the pain in her hand. Then, feeling light-headed, she dashes up the stairs two by two until she gets to Buster's room.

He is curled up on his bed with his back to her, gray and pale. "Go away!" he grumbles, his voice twisted in hurt and sadness.

"Buster!" Polly says. "Buster! I've been a terrible friend and I'm sorry, I really am. But you have to listen to me right now. There are witches at the door that will hurt you if they can get to you. We have to get away."

Polly rushes to the window and looks out into Buster's garden. The witches have surrounded the house. Deidre Halloway is below the window and when she sees Polly's face, she shrieks, "Polly! Let us in! You are in danger! We know there are dangerous monsters in that house. Let us in! Let us in!"

Polly looks down at the bite wound on her hand. She knows this is all the proof that horrible Mrs. Halloway is looking for. They might even say it was *Buster* who bit her! Polly shudders at the thought. She can never let those witches get in.

This is all her fault. Buster has only ever been a friend to her, and now their friendship has put him in danger. Those witches would never be here, at Buster's house, if it weren't for her!

She feels anger boil inside her as she pushes open the window and climbs out onto the windowsill.

"It's not true! None of it is true, and you know it!" she shouts at the huddle of witches below. "It wasn't your daughter I was protecting with that spell in the gallery, Mrs. Halloway. It was Buster, my friend. My *best* friend! But you and Malorie twisted the whole story around to make witches hate monsters even more. The only dangerous thing in this town is *you*, and your horrible Committee. I am going to make sure every witch and warlock in this town knows it!"

"Polly Proggett, you *will* let us in!" Mrs. Halloway hisses, her face blooming red with rage.

As Polly watches, Mrs. Halloway dips her hand into her cape and pulls out a wand. She points it up at Polly. The witches on either side of her gasp and jump back.

"No!"

Polly shouts, and before she realizes what is happening, the anger that started deep in her belly has bubbled right up into her chest, through her lungs and up into her head.

Stop! Polly thinks to herself, but it is too late.

Little sparks begin shooting out of her fingertips. She tries to calm herself, but she is too angry, too ferocious, and a jolt like electricity passes from her toes to her head.

A flash of light

erupts from her fingertips

and spreads toward the scowling witches below, who are all thrown to the ground.

Polly feels her head grow fuzzy and her body crumples, falling into the darkness below.

Twenty

Polly has only passed out for a moment, but when she wakes, she senses something very strange has happened. She has her cheek against Buster's fur and he has his arms wrapped tightly around her. All around them is the night sky.

She feels like she is floating upward, and when she opens her eyes she sees that, sure enough, the ground is far below them.

"Buster," she croaks,
but he is busy humming
and doesn't answer.
When she looks up at him, he smiles, and she
sees he is as big as a rowboat and as pink as a
cherry. And as light as a blossom on the wind.

They are floating **up, up, up**
into the starry sky.

Buster stops humming
and begins to sing,
"Me and you, you
and me, that's the way
it will always be …"

It's the song they invented
when they were younger.

Polly understands. She has been forgiven,
and that's all that matters.

Twenty-One

They are high in the sky now. Polly knows that with one moment of doubt or fear, they could both plummet to the ground.

Polly begins to sing along with Buster. She knows they need their **happy song** to help Buster stay up.

They float above treetops and church steeples, and when Polly dares to look down, she sees people, like tiny matchsticks, pointing and waving and running along the streets below them. The sound of their shouting is now too far away to be heard.

Up ahead is the clock tower of the Town Hall, and this gives Polly an idea. It has a nice flat top she is sure is big enough for the two of them. Gradually she stops singing. Buster looks around like he is waking from a dream and Polly sees doubt flood through him.

"Oh, I didn't realize we were so high!" he says, and immediately he begins to shrink.

"Slowly, slowly, Buster!" Polly urges, as they begin to fall. "We'll be OK. Look! There is somewhere for us to land, just up ahead.

Think happy thoughts for a little while longer.
Snow angels!" she cries.

"And cuddles!
Moonberry
cake!

And bluebirds! You love bluebirds!"

"I do," says Buster wistfully. "And yellow ones."

"That's right," Polly says, as they begin to float upward again. "And pink ones and green ones. All kinds of pretty birds singing at your window when you wake in the morning. And it's sunny outside."

Buster smiles. "And you are in the tree, waiting for me."

"As it'll always be," says Polly.

She leans her head against Buster's chest as they drift slowly down onto the roof of the clock tower, landing gently just as Buster shrinks back to his normal size.

It's cold up so high. The wind is fierce and it has begun to drizzle. Polly shivers, so Buster wraps his big hairy arms around her like a fur coat and sits with his back to the wind.

"I'm so tired," Polly rasps, her throat sore from all the singing, and her head still spinning from the spell.

Buster strokes her hair with his big paw.

"You came to rescue me," he says. "Little witch Polly standing up for big old Buster the monster again. That made me so happy."

"You rescued me, too," Polly murmurs. She peers down over the edge of the clock tower. "I don't know who is going to rescue us now, though."

Her head has stopped spinning, but now it's aching from the spell. And her hand is throbbing where Maggie bit her. It's all she can do to close her eyes and breathe through the pain.

"Polly?" Buster whispers. "Polly, I think someone's coming." She hears his heart begin to beat faster. "On a broomstick," he says nervously.

Polly opens her eyes and there, not far in the

distance, is a witch speeding toward them on her broomstick, long hair snaking out from her tall black hat, her cape flapping behind her. She's flying higher than Polly has ever seen a witch fly. Polly gasps when she recognizes who it is.

"Miss Spinnaker!"

Miss Spinnaker screeches to a halt

and hovers just beside the clock tower, her cheeks red and her eyes bright from the cold. Her hair, freed from her usual messy bun, whips about her face in the wind and the rain.

"Well, why am I not surprised to find it is *you* up here, Polly Proggett?" she says, raising her arched eyebrows high. "It seems that trouble has a habit of following you about these days, doesn't it?"

"Polly rescued me from the mean witches," Buster says, pulling her in tighter toward him. "Don't be cross with her."

"Oh," says Miss Spinnaker, looking at Polly a little more closely. "You've been bitten!"

Buster notices the bite for the first time. "Polly!" he says. "Was that Maggie?"

"It's OK, she didn't mean it," Polly says quickly. "She just got a fright when those witches came banging on the door looking for Buster. They scared her."

Miss Spinnaker nods. Polly can see her teacher is putting everything together without her having to explain it all, and at that moment she loves Miss Spinnaker more than ever.

"Well," she says, "we'd best get that fixed up before Mrs. Halloway finds out. On you hop," she says, patting the broomstick behind her. "You'd both better come back to my place so I can fix you up before you go home."

Twenty-Two

Within minutes, Miss Spinnaker pulls up in front of a little white cottage with a garden full of herbs and a crooked front gate.

They follow Polly's teacher into the house and down the little hallway into the kitchen. It's the first time Polly has ever been in her teacher's house, and for some reason it makes her feel embarrassed. Like she has just caught a glimpse of Miss Spinnaker in her underwear or something.

Polly looks around the tiny kitchen. It is perfectly neat, but crowded with wonderful trinkets and floral teacups and newspapers and books piled up carefully.

At school, Miss Spinnaker seems so gracious and wise, so Polly had always imagined she might live somewhere very grand, like a palace. Not a little white cottage with a herb garden and a crooked front gate.

Miss Spinnaker gestures toward the rickety wooden table, and turns to the stove to put an old iron kettle on to boil. A sleek black cat jumps up onto the counter and Miss Spinnaker runs her hand down his body and kisses the top of his head.

Polly and Buster sit down. There is a bowl of ripe ju-ju fruits on the table and Buster stares at them longingly.

"Help yourself," Miss Spinnaker says, as she jangles over to inspect Polly's wound more closely.

Buster takes three, but Polly gives him a dark look, so he puts one back in the bowl.

Polly is impressed at how different her teacher looks out of the classroom and after her broomstick ride. Her long red hair is **wild** and her green eyes **flash** like emeralds.

Just like a real Black Witch, Polly thinks admiringly.

"Now, let's have a better look at this wound," Miss Spinnaker says, peering down at Polly's hand. The skin around the puncture marks is red and swollen. "A monster's bite can become infected very quickly if left untreated," she explains. "Just as well she didn't bite you harder. She could have taken your whole hand off!"

"It's really not a serious bite," says Polly.

Miss Spinnaker puts a hand on Polly's

forehead. "All the same, you have a slight fever already."

"She did another spell, too," Buster says, his mouth full of ju-ju fruit. Purple juice trickles down his chin.

"**Polly!**" says Miss Spinnaker. She frowns and puts both hands on her hips.

"It just came out of me," Polly whimpers. "I didn't mean to. Mrs. Halloway pointed a wand at me!"

Miss Spinnaker gasps. "What?" She shakes her head and her mouth sets into a hard line. "A fully grown witch pointing a wand at a child? What is this world coming to?"

"I did try to stop the spell from coming out,"

Polly says. "But I was scared and angry …"

"She was protecting me again," Buster says, leaning his head affectionately on Polly's shoulder and sucking purple juice off his fingers.

"It wasn't as big as the one in the gallery," Polly continues.

"Polly. That's two spells out of school grounds now. You know very well what three means?"

Polly hangs her head. "I know," she says. "Expelled from school."

Miss Spinnaker nods. Then she softens. "Well, at least you appear to be less affected this time. That's a good sign, I suppose. It hopefully means you'll be able to control yourself soon. I would hate to see you expelled from the Academy."

She bustles over to a wide cupboard by the sink. Inside are dozens of tiny glass jars of all different shapes, colors and sizes, filled with all manner of strange ingredients.

Miss Spinnaker hesitates for a moment, then pulls out five little bottles and carries them over to a big black cauldron sitting on her kitchen counter. She shoos the cat away and he jumps down onto the floor.

"Actually, I have been thinking a lot about you lately." She turns to look at Polly again.

"I am not absolutely sure, but I have a strong feeling you might be a Silver Witch."

Polly scrunches up her face. "A *Silver* Witch?"

"Cool!" says Buster, and he reaches for another fruit.

"Buster!" Polly whispers. "You've already had *two!*"

Buster puts his hands back on his lap.

Miss Spinnaker unplugs a glass stopper from each bottle and carefully measures out ingredients into a beaker before tipping them into the cauldron. Polly recognizes grout juice and bramble mix, as well as thistle weed and ground seaswell, but she can't make out what the other things are.

Miss Spinnaker carries the cauldron over to the fireplace and hooks it up over the flames.

"Did your father ever give you anything special before he died?" Miss Spinnaker asks, stirring the mixture with a long wooden spoon.

A swirl of different images flit through Polly's mind. The star stickers. A tricycle. Dragon beads. Polly shakes her head. Nothing in particular is coming to her, but the memories rushing into her mind squeeze at her heart.

Miss Spinnaker stirs slowly, staring down into the pot. Steam has begun to rise up into the chimney. "No? Nothing precious, that he told you to keep always?"

She turns to Polly and smiles as if she knows the answer already.

Polly looks into her teacher's eyes and suddenly she knows what it is, too.

Twenty-Three

Polly hears her father's voice. Sees his kind face. She reaches into her pocket, her fingers touching the smooth silk of the little pouch hidden in there. She thinks about how insistent her mother was that the pouch of stones was for Polly to keep. Polly, and no one else.

She draws it out slowly and tips the three stones onto her palm. They **gleam** gently in the bright kitchen light.

"Aren't they from me?" Buster asks hopefully.

He pulls a couple of pebbles out from his front pocket and lays them down on the table. Then he pulls out a piece of bark and a stick, and puts them next to the stones. Just in case they might be special, too.

Miss Spinnaker scoops some of the bubbling gray mixture from the cauldron into a small white bowl. Then she pulls out a packet of bandages from a cupboard above the stove and hurries back over to Polly.

While she waits for the healing potion to cool, she studies Polly and Buster's stone collections.

"Those are lovely stones, Buster," she says kindly, but it's clear she isn't really paying any attention to his collection of treasures.

Buster sighs a little in disappointment.

It's Polly's stones that make her teacher's eyes gleam. "Hmmm. You do know what these are, don't you, Polly?" she says, unable to hide the excitement in her voice.

She passes her hand over the three stones and they begin to glow.

"Wow," says Buster. "They *are* special stones!" He pokes at his small brown stones, which now look particularly ordinary.

"I have activated these stones, Polly," says Miss Spinnaker, "but I can't touch them. Only you can, because they were given to you. Pick them up."

Polly does as she is told. She is surprised to feel how warm they have become.

"Good. Hold them tight in your palm and close your eyes. They will tell you what you need to do."

Miss Spinnaker pulls up a chair and sits down beside Polly. She puts her hand on Polly's shoulder. "I should warn you that this might feel a little frightening at first. You'll get used to it, but the first time can feel a little … scary. Like your first spell. And you might feel a bit sick afterward. But don't worry, I'll be right here beside you."

Polly closes her eyes. The stones in her palm grow warmer and warmer. Soon, she feels the heat travel into her skin, up her arm and into the rest of her body.

"Well done, Polly," she hears Miss Spinnaker say. "Now just relax and focus on what comes into your mind."

Polly feels Miss Spinnaker's cat weave between her legs but she brings her focus back to the stones. Her head becomes full of images. They flash in front of her eyes one by one, faster and faster. She hears her blood **throbbing** in her ears. This is nothing like dreaming, nothing like imagination. It's like watching a film she can't turn off.

Her breath becomes faster and the stones grow hotter and hotter in her palm. Suddenly they become too hot to hold, and Polly drops them onto the table as her eyes spring open. She is panting, and sweat trickles down the sides of her forehead.

"Good work, Polly," Miss Spinnaker says. "You are very brave to have stayed in there so long."

Polly looks at her teacher. Her heart is still pounding. "It's up to me, isn't it?" she gasps. Her skin is covered in goose bumps and her stomach is beginning to curl.

Miss Spinnaker takes her hand to encourage her to go on. Polly doesn't know if she is more terrified or more thrilled.

"It's up to me. I started this. With the spell in the gallery. I started this war of witches against monsters. It's up to me to stop it now, isn't it?"

Polly's teacher nods slowly. "If that's what the stones told you then I'm afraid so, Polly. Every generation has a Silver Witch who is uncovered just when she is needed. I had an inkling it might be you. I took the day off school today to meditate on who it might be. Your face kept coming into my mind. Even so, I really didn't think it could be someone so young. And someone so … unpracticed!"

She stirs the small bowl of healing potion on the table. As it cools, it has begun to thicken. Miss Spinnaker scoops out a blob of the gray goop and smears it across the wound on Polly's hand.

"It can't be me," Polly says. "I'm hopeless at … everything!"

"The stones don't lie, Polly," Miss Spinnaker says, wrapping Polly's hand in gauze. "If they say it is you, it is you."

"Maybe I didn't understand them properly?" Polly says. "You would be *much* better at this sort of thing than me. I can try again, if you like?"

Miss Spinnaker smiles and cups Polly's cheek. "Polly, it's *you*. You've always been a bit … different. And now I see why! Look, maybe this was brought on a little earlier by your spell at the gallery, but this conflict between witches and monsters has been heating up for a long time now. Don't worry, I will support you as best as I can. And the stones will guide you the rest of the way. I can train you to use your spells more effectively, and teach you some basic potions."

She looks up at Polly and her eyes crease into a mischievous smile. "Though you might need to work on your temper."

Polly chews her bottom lip nervously. "I'm scared," she admits.

"Of course you are!" Miss Spinnaker says. "Gosh, that's completely understandable! I imagine some of the things the stones showed you might have been terrifying. But every Silver Witch has a companion. Someone you can trust. You might have seen them in your visions, framed in a white light. Did anyone like that come into your mind, Polly?" she asks.

Polly frowns, and tries to think back.

"There *was* a white light," she remembers. "And there was someone in it." Polly pauses, closing her eyes for a moment. "I don't think it was a witch, though. Actually, I think it may have been a monster. Oh! Yes, I remember now. It *was* a monster. A big, *hairy* monster …"

Miss Spinnaker and Polly turn to look at Buster. He has snuck another ju-ju fruit out of the bowl and jammed the whole thing into his mouth. Juice dribbles down his furry chin. When he feels both witches' eyes on him, he slowly stops chewing and wipes his chin on the back of his paw.

"**Wha–?**" he says, blushing. "Miss Spinnaker *said* I could help myself. Ohhhhh," he says, finally realizing why they are staring at him. "*I'm* a big hairy monster!"

Polly grins. She is terrified of what lies ahead, and is absolutely certain there is no way anything Miss Spinnaker can teach her will make her strong enough, or clever enough, or brave enough.

But somehow, knowing
Buster will be by her side
makes everything
feel OK.

Acknowledgements

If I had to squeeze all the people into my heart that I needed to thank for helping me bring this book into the world, it would explode into a million pieces and the room would be covered in heart bits and muck, so it's probably much safer I just try to list them all here.

Everyone at Hardie Grant Egmont is my absolute favorite person: Annabel, Marisa, Penny, Amanda, Sarah, Charlotte, Ilka, Haylee, Mandy – and anyone else I may have overlooked in my excitable typing. It's a joy to work with such talented, enthusiastic, gorgeous ladies. I couldn't imagine being in better hands. But of course I must give special mention to Hilary Rogers, publisher, midwife, hand-holder and book whisperer who has been there for Polly and Buster from the beginning.

Pippa Masson is my constant champion, as is Davina Bell, who I want to bundle up and bottle for all the sparkling gorgeousness that she is. I could never thank her enough for hot chai on a cold beach, old lady yoga sessions and the winery writers' retreats where this book began to take shape. She also gives the best manuscript feedback around.

I am beyond excited that the completely brilliant Stephanie Spartels agreed to design this book. I am such a massive fan of her work and as far as I am concerned she has made true magic happen across these pages.

My very first readers big and small deserve monster-sized thanks: Fiona Harris and Scott Edgar, as well as Nellie Edgar who chatted with me about witches and monsters over ice-cream and whose daddy helped me get my drawing mojo back. Tilly, Tessa and Ollie listened to me read parts of this aloud and laughed uproariously in all the right places and Dom carries my heart into the world.

My mother, who has somehow become my accountant, life organiser and career advisor all in one, but who, even more importantly, said to me those very words that Buster's mother does to Polly: *"It's all very well to love those who are loveable, but it's the unloveable ones who need it the most."* She is a beacon of generosity and kindness.

Lastly, Buster is Polly's dearest, loveliest friend who is there for her through everything: sad when she is sad, joyful in her joy. If you ever find a friend like this, hold onto them tight because there is no greater treasure in the world. I have many beautiful friends who sparkle like stars and guide me when I need it most. But I have only one Buster, and I intend to hold onto him as close and as long as time will allow.

About Sally Rippin

Sally Rippin is the sort of grown-up who remembers exactly what it was like to be a kid. That's one of the reasons her books are so beloved around the world. She has written more than sixty books for children, including the best-selling *Billie B. Brown* and *Hey Jack!*. Sally's books have sold over four million copies internationally, which is enough to make any monster puff up with happiness.